Affectionately to my Father,

The Reverend GRIGG THOMPSON.

By MAURICE THOMPSON.

NEW YORK:
E. J. HALE & SON, PUBLISHERS,
MURRAY STREET.
1875.

CONTENTS.

Was She a Boy?

No matter what business or what pleasure took me, I once, not long ago, went to Colfax. Whisper it not to each other that I was seeking a foreign appointment through the influence of my fellow Hoosier, the late Vice-President of the United States. O no, I didn't go to the Hon. Schuyler Colfax at all; but I went to Colfax, simply, which is a little dingy town, in Clinton County, that was formerly called Midway, because it is half way between Lafayette and Indianapolis. It was and is a place of some three hundred inhabitants, eking out an aguish subsistence, maintaining a swampy, malarious aspect, keeping up a bilious, nay, an atra-bilious color, the year round, by sucking like an attenuated leech at the junction, or, rather, the crossing of the I. C. & L., and the L. C. & S. W. railroads. It lay mouldering, like something lost and forgotten, slowly rotting in the swamp.

I do not mean to attack the inhabitants of

Colfax, for they were good people, and deserved a better fate than the eternal rattling the ague took them through from year's end to year's end. Why, they had had the ague so long that they had no respect for it at all. I've seen a woman in Colfax shaking with a chill, spanking a baby that had a chill, and scolding a husband who had a chill, all at once—and I had a dreadful ague on me at the same time! But, as I have said, they were good people, and I suppose they are still. They go quietly about the usual business of dead towns. They have "stores" in which they offer for sale calico, of the big-figured, orange and red sort, surprisingly cheap. They smoke those little Cuba sixes at a half cent apiece, and call them cigars; they hang round the dépôt, and trade jack-knives and lottery watches on the afternoons of lazy Sundays; they make harmless sport of the incoming and outgoing country folk; and, in a word, keep pretty busy at one thing or another, and above all—they shake.

In Colfax the chief sources of exciting amusement are dog fights and an occasional row at Sheehan's saloon, a doggery of the regular old-fashioned, drink, gamble, rob and fight sort—a low place, known to all the hard bats in the State.

As you pass through the town you will not fail to notice a big sign, outhanging from the front of the largest building on the principal street, which reads: "Union Hotel, 1865." From the muddy suburbs of the place, in every direction, stretch black muck swamps, for the most part heavily timbered with a variety of oaks, interspersed with sycamores, ash, and elms. In the damp, shady labyrinths of these boggy woods millions of lively, wide awake, tuneful mosquitoes are daily manufactured; and out from decaying logs and piles of fermenting leaves, from the green pools and sluggish ditch streams, creeps a noxious gas, known in that region as the "double refined, high pressure, forty hoss power quintessential of the ager!" So, at least, I was told by the landlord of the Union Hotel, and his skin had the color of one who knew.

Notwithstanding what I have said, Colfax, in summer, is not wholly without attractions of a certain kind. It has some yellow dogs and some brindle ones; it has some cattle and some swine; it has some swallows and some spotted pigeons; it has cool, fresh smelling winds, and, after the water has sufficiently dried out, the woods are really glorious with wild roses, violets, turkey-pea blossoms, and wild pinks. But to my story.

I was sitting on the long veranda of the Union Hotel, when a rough but kindly voice said to me:

"Mornin', stranger; gi' me a light, will ye?"

I looked up from the miserable dime novel at which I had been tugging for the last hour, and saw before me a corpulent man of, perhaps, forty-five years of age, who stood quite ready to thrust the charred end of a cigar stump into the bowl of my meerschaum. I gave him a match, and would fain have returned to Angelina St. Fortescue, the heroine of the novel, whom I had left standing on the extreme giddy verge of a sheer Alpine precipice, known, by actual triangulation, to be just seven thousand feet high, swearing she would leap off if Donald Gougerizeout, the robber, persisted further in his rough addresses; but my new friend, the corpulent smoker, seemed bent on a little bit of conversation.

"Thankee, sir. Fine mornin', sir, a'n't it?"

"Beautiful," I replied, raising my head, elevating my arms, and, by a kind of yawn, taking in a deep draught of the fresh spring weather, absorbing it, assimilating it, till, like a wave of retarded electricity, it set my nerves in tune for enjoying the bird songs, and filled my blood with the ecstasy of vigorous health and youth. I, no doubt, just then felt the burden of life much less than did the big yellow dog at my feet, who snapped lazily at the flies.

"Yes, yes, this 'ere's a fine mornin'—julicious, sir, julicious, indeed; but le' me tell ye, sir, this 'ere wind's mighty deceitful—for a fact it is, sir, jist as full of ager as a acorn is of meat. It's blowin' right off'n ponds, and is loaded chock down with the miasm—for a fact it is, sir."

While delivering this speech, the fat man sat down on the bench beside me there in the veranda. By this time I had my thumbs in the arm holes of my vest, and my chest expanded to its utmost—my lungs going like a steam bellows, which is a way I have in fine weather.

"Monstrous set o' respiratory organs, them o' your'n," he said, eyeing my manœuvres. Just then I discovered that he was a physician of the steam doctor sort, for, glancing down at my feet, I espied his well worn leather medicine bags. I immediately grew polite. Possibly I might ere long need some quinine, or mandrake, or a hot steam bath—anything for the ague!

"Yes, I've got lungs like a porpoise," I replied, "but still the ague may get me. Much sickness about here, Doctor——a——a—— what do they call your name?"

"Benjamin Hurd—Doctor Hurd, they call me. I'm the only thorer bred botanic that's in these parts. I do poorty much all the practice about here. Yes, there's considerable of ager and phthisic and bilious fever. Keeps me busy most of my time. These nasty swamps, you know."

After a time our conversation flagged, and the doctor having lit a fresh cigar, we smoked in silence. The wind was driving the dust along the street in heavy waves, and I sat watching a couple of lean, spotted calves making their way against the tide. They held their heads low and shut their eyes, now and then bawling vigorously. Some one up stairs was playing "Days of Absence" on a wretched wheezing accordeon.

"There's a case of asthma, doctor," I said, intending to be witty. But my remark was not noticed. The doctor was in a brown study, from which my words had not startled him. Presently he said, as if talking to himself, and without taking the cigar from his mouth:

"'Twas just a year ago to-night, the 28th

day of May, 'at they took 'er away. And he'll die afore day to a dead certainty. Beats all the derned queer things I ever seed or heerd of."

He was poking with the toe of his boot in the dust on the veranda floor, as he spoke, and stealing a glance at his face, I saw that it wore an abstracted, dreamy, perplexed look.

"What was your remark, doctor?" I asked, more to arouse him than from any hope of being interested.

"Hum!—ah, yes," he said, starting, and beginning a vigorous puffing. "Ah, yes, I was cogitatin' over this matter o' Berry Young's. Never have been able to 'count for that, no how. Think about it more an' more every day. What's your theory of it?"

"Can't say, never having heard anything of it," I replied.

"Well, I do say! Thought everybody had hearn of that, any how! It's a rale romance, a reg'lar mystery, sir. It's been talked about, and writ about in the papers so much 'at I s'posed 'at it was knowed of far and wide."

"I've been in California for several years past," I replied, by way of excuse for my ignorance of even the vaguest outline of the affair, whatever it might be.

"Well, you see, a leetle more'n a year ago a gal an' her father come here and stopped at this 'ere very hotel. The man must 'a' been som'res near sixty years old; but the gal was young, and jist the poortiest thing I ever seed in all my life. I couldn't describe how she looked at all; but everybody 'at saw her said she was the beautifulest creatur they ever laid eyes onto. Where these two folks come from nobody ever knowed, but they seemed like mighty nice sort of persons, and everybody liked 'em, 'specially the gal. Somehow, from the very start, a kind of mystery hung 'round 'em. They seemed always to have gobs o' money, and onct in awhile some little thing'd turn up to make folks kinder juberous somehow 'at they wasn't jist what they ginerally seemed to be. But that gal was fascinatin' as a snake, and as poorty as any picter. Her flesh looked like tinted wax mixed with moonshine, and her eyes was as clear as a limestone spring — though they was dark as night. She was that full of restless animal life 'at she couldn't set still—she roamed round like a leopard in a cage, and she'd romp equal to a ten-year-old boy. Well, as mought be expected, sich a gal as that 'ere 'd 'tract attention in these parts, and I must say 'at the young fellows here did git 'bominable sweet on her. 'Casionally two of 'em 'd git out in the swamps and have a awful fight on her 'count; but she 'peared to pay precious little 'tention to any of 'em till finally Berry Young stepped in and jist went for 'er like mad, and she took to 'm. Berry was r'ally the nicest and intelligentest young man in all this country. He writ poetry for the papers, sir—snatchin' good poetry, too—and had got to be talked of a right smart for his larnin', an' 'compiishments. He was good lookin', too; powerful handsome, for a fact, sir. So they was to be married, Berry and the gal, an' the time it was sot, an' the day it come, an' all was ready, an' the young folks was on the floor, and the 'squire was jist a commencin' to say the ceremony, when lo! and beholden, four big, awful, rough lookin' men rushed in with big pistols and mighty terrible bowie knives, and big papers and big seals, and said they was a sheriff and possum from Kaintucky. They jist jumped right onto the gal an' her father an' han'cuffed 'em, an' took 'em!"

"Handcuffed them and took them!" I repeated, suddenly growing intensely interested. This was beating my dime novel, for sensation, all hollow.

"Yes, sir, han'cuffed 'em an' took 'em, an' away they went, an' they've not been hearn of since to this day. But the mysteriousest thing about the whole business was that when the sheriff grabbed the gal he called her George, and said she wasn't no gal at all, but jist a terrible onery boy 'at had been stealin' an' counterfeitin' an' robbin' all round everywhere. What d'ye think of that?"

"A remarkably strange affair, certainly," I replied; "and do you say that the father and the girl have not since been heard from?"

"Never a breath. The thing got into all the newspapers and raised a awful rumpus, and it turned out that it wasn't no sheriff 'at come there; but some dark, mysterious kidnappin' transaction 'at nobody could account for. Detectives was put on their track an' follered 'em to Injun territory an' there lost 'em. Some big robberies was connected with the affair, but folks could never git head nor tail of the partic'lers."

"And it wasn't a real sheriff's arrest, then?" said I.

"No, sir, 'twas jist a mystery. Some kind of a dodge of a band of desperadoes to avoid the law some way. The papers tried to explain it, but I never could see any sense to it. 'Twas a clean, dead mystery. But I was goin' on to tell ye 'at Berry Young took it awful hard 'bout the gal, an' he's been sort o' sinkin' away ever sence, an' now he's jist ready to wink out. Yonder's where Berry lives, in that 'ere white cottage house with the vines round the winder. He's desp'rit sick—a sort o' consumption. I'm goin' to see 'im now; good mornin' to ye."

Thus abruptly ending our interview, the doctor took up his medicine bag and went his way. He left me in a really excited state of mind; the story of itself was so strange, and the narrator had told it so solemnly and graphically. I suppose, too, that I must have been in just the proper state of mind for that rough outline, that cartoon of a most startling and mysterious affair, to become deeply impressed in my mind, perhaps, in the most fascinating and fantastic light possible. A thirst to know more of the story took strong hold on my mind, as if I had been reading a tantalizing romance and had found the leaves torn out just where the mystery was to be explained. I half closed my eyes to better keep in the lines and shades of the strange picture. Its influence lay upon me like a spell. I enjoyed it. It was a luxury.

The wings of the morning wind fanned the

heat into broken waves, rising and sinking, and flowing on, with murmur and flash and glimmer, to the cool green ways of the woods, and, like the wind, my fancy went out among golden fleece clouds and into shady places, following the thread of this new romance. I cannot give a sufficient reason why the story took so fast a hold on me. But it did grip my mind and master it. It appeared to me the most intensely strange affair I had ever heard of.

While I sat there, lost in reflection, with my eyes bent on a very unpromising pig, that wallowed in the damp earth by the town pump, the landlord of the hotel came out and took a seat beside me. I gave him a pipe of my tobacco and forthwith began plying him with questions touching the affair of which the doctor had spoken. He confirmed the story, and added to its mystery by going minutely into its details. He gave the names of the father and daughter as Charles Afton and Ollie Afton.

Ollie Afton! Certainly no name sounds sweeter! How is it that these gifted, mysteriously beautiful persons always have musical names!

"Ah," said the landlord, "you'd ort to have seen that boy!"

"Boy!" I echoed.

"Well, gal or boy, one or t'other, the wonderfulest human bein' I ever see in all the days o' my life! Lips as red as ripe cur'n's, and for ever smilin'. Such smiles—oonkoo! they hurt a feller all over, they was so sweet. She was tall an' dark, an' had black hair that curled short all 'round her head. Her skin was wonderful clear and so was her eyes. But it was the way she looked at you that got you. Ah, sir, she had a power in them eyes, to be sure!"

The pig got up from his muddy place by the pump, grunted, as if satisfied, and slowly strolled off; a country lad drove past, riding astride the hounds of a wagon; a pigeon lit on the comb of the roof of Sheehan's saloon, which was just across the street, and began pluming itself. Just then the landlord's little sharp-nosed, weasel-eyed boy came out and said, in a very subdued tone of voice:

"Pap, mam says 'at if you don't kill 'er that 'ere chicken for dinner you kin go widout any fing to eat all she cares."

The landlord's spouse was a red-headed woman, so he got up very suddenly and took himself into the house. But before he got out of hearing the little boy remarked:

"Pap, I speaks for the gizzard of that 'ere chicken, d'ye hear, now?"

I sat there till the dinner hour, watching the soft pink and white vapors that rolled round the verge of the horizon. I was thoroughly saturated with romance. Strange, that here, in this dingy little out-of-the-way village, should have transpired one of the most wonderful mysteries history may ever hold!

At dinner the landlord talked volubly of the Afton affair, giving it as his opinion that the Aftons were persons tinged with negro blood, and had been kidnapped into slavery.

"They was jist as white, an' whiter, too, than I am," he went on, "but them Southerners 'd jist as soon sell one person as 'nother, anyhow."

I noticed particularly that the little boy got his choice bit of the fowl. He turned his head one side and ate like a cat.

When the meal was over I was again joined by Doctor Hurd on the verandah. He reported Berry Young still alive, but not able to live till midnight. I noticed that the doctor was nervous and kept his eyes fixed on Sheehan's saloon.

"Stranger," said he, leaning over close to me, and speaking in a low, guarded way, "things is workin' dasted curious 'bout now—sure's gun's iron they jist is!"

"Where—how—in what way, doctor?" I stammered, taken aback by his behavior.

"Sumpum's up, as sure as Ned!" he replied, wagging his head.

"Doctor," I said, petulantly, "if you would be a trifle more explicit I could probably guess, with some show of certainty, at what you mean!"

"Can't ye hear? Are ye deaf? Did ye ever, in all yer born days, hear a voice like that ere 'un? Listen!"

Sure enough, a voice of thrilling power, a rich, heavy, quavering alto, accompanied by some one thrumming on a guitar, trickled and gurgled, and poured through the open window of Sheehan's saloon. The song was a wild, drinking carol, full of rough, reckless wit, but I listened, entranced, till it was done.

"There now, say, what d'ye think o' that? Ain't things a workin' round awful curious, as I said?"

Delivering himself thus, the doctor got up and walked off.

When I again had an opportunity to speak to the landlord, I asked him if Doctor Hurd was not thought to be slightly demented.

"What! crazy, do you mean? No, sir; bright as a pin!"

"Well," said I, "he's a very queer fellow any how. By the way, who was that singing just now over in the saloon there?"

"Don't know, didn't hear 'em. Some of the boys, I s'pose. They have some lively swells over there sometimes. Awful hole."

I resumed my dime novel, and nothing further transpired to aggravate or satisfy my curiosity concerning the strange story I had heard, till night came down and the bats began to wheel through the moonless blackness above the dingy town. At the coming on of dusk I flung away the book and took to my pipe. Some one touched me on the shoulder, rousing me from a deep reverie, if not a doze.

"Ha, stranger, this you, eh? Berry Young's a dyin'; go over there wi' me, will ye?"

It was the voice of Doctor Hurd.

"What need for me have you?" I replied, rather stiffly, not much relishing this too obtrusive familiarity.

"Well—I—I jist kinder wanted ye to go over. The poor boy's 'bout passin' away, an' things is a workin' so tarnation curious! Come 'long wi' me, friend, will ye?"

Something in the fellow's voice touched me,

and without another word I arose and followed him to the cottage. The night was intensely black. I think it was clear, but a heavy fog from the swamps had settled over everything, and through this dismal veil the voices of owls from far and near struck with hollow, sepulchral effect.

"A heart is the trump!" sang out that alto voice from within the saloon as we passed.

Doctor Hurd clutched my arm and muttered:

"That's that voice ag'in! Strange—strange! Poor Berry Young!"

We entered the cottage and found ourselves in a cosy little room, where, on a low bed, a pale, intelligent looking young man lay, evidently dying. He was very much emaciated, his eyes, wonderfully large and luminous, were sunken, and his breathing quick and difficult. A haggard, watching-worn woman sat by his bed. From her resemblance to him I took her to be his sister. She was evidently very unwell herself. We sat in silence by his bedside, watching his life flow into eternity, till the little clock on the mantel struck, sharp and clear, the hour of ten.

The sound of the bell startled the sick man, and after some incoherent mumbling he said, quite distinctly:

"Sister, if you ever again see Ollie Afton, tell him—tell her—tell, say I forgive him—say to her—him—I loved her all my life—tell him—ah! what was I saying? Don't cry, sis, please. What a sweet, faithful sister! Ah! it's almost over, dear—— Ah, me!"

For some minutes the sister's sobbing echoed strangely through the house. The dying man drew his head far down in the soft pillow. A breath of damp air stole through the room.

All at once, right under the window by which the bed sat, arose a touching guitar prelude—a tangled mesh of melody—gusty, throbbing, wandering through the room and straying off into the night, tossing back its trembling echoes fainter and fainter, till, as it began to die, that same splendid alto voice caught the key and flooded the darkness with song. The sick man raised himself on his elbow, and his face flashed out the terrible smile of death. He listened eagerly. It was the song "Come Where my Love lies Dreaming," but who has heard it rendered as it was that night? Every chord of the voice was as sweet and witching as a wind harp's, and the low, humming undertone of the accompaniment was perfection. Tenderly but awfully sweet, the music at length faded into utter silence, and Berry Young sank limp and pallid upon his pillows.

"It is Ollie," he hoarsely whispered. "Tell her—tell him—O say to her for me—ah! water, sis, it's all over!"

The woman hastened, but before she could get the water to his lips he was dead. His last word was Ollie.

The sister cast herself upon the dead man's bosom and sobbed wildly, piteously. Soon after this some neighbors came in, which gave me an opportunity to quietly take my leave.

The night was so foggy and dark that, but for a bright stream of light from a window of Sheehan's saloon, it would have been hard for me to find my way back to the hotel. I did find it, however, and sat down upon the verandah. I had nearly fallen asleep, thinking over the strange occurrences of the past few hours, when the rumble of an approaching train of cars on the I. C. & L. from the east aroused me, and, at the same moment, a great noise began over in the saloon. High words, a few bitter oaths, a struggle as of persons fighting, a loud, sonorous crash like the crushing of a musical instrument, and then I saw the burly bar tender hurl some one out through the doorway just as the express train stopped close by.

"All aboard!" cried the conductor, waving

his lantern. At the same time, as the bar-tender stood in the light of his doorway, a brickbat, whizzing from the darkness, struck him full in the face, knocking him precipitately back at full length on to the floor of the saloon.

"All aboard!" repeated the conductor.

"All aboard!" jeeringly echoed a delicious alto voice; and I saw a slender man step up on the rear platform of the smoking car. A flash from the conductor's lantern lit up for a moment this fellow's face, and it was the most beautiful visage I have ever seen. Extremely youthful, dark, resplendent, glorious, set round with waves and ringlets of black hair—it was such a countenance as I have imagined a young Chaldean might have had who was destined to the high calling of astrology. It was a face to charm, to electrify the beholder with its indescribable, almost unearthly loveliness of features and expression.

The engine whistled, the bell rang, and as the train moved on, that slender, almost fragile form and wonderful face disappeared in the darkness.

As the roar and clash of the receding cars began to grow faint in the distance, a gurgling, grunting sound over in the saloon reminded me that the bar-tender might need some attention, so I stepped across the street and went in. He was just taking himself up from the floor, with his nose badly smashed, spurting blood over him pretty freely. He was in an ecstasy of fury and swore fearfully. I rendered him all the aid I could, getting the blood stopped, at length, and a plaster over the wound.

"Who struck you?" I asked.

"Who struck me? Who hit me with that 'ere brick, d'ye say? Who but that little baby-faced, hawk-eyed cuss 'at got off here yesterday! He's a thief and a dog!—he's chowzed me out'n my last cent! Where is he?—I'll kill 'im yet! where is he?"

"Gone off on the train," I replied, "but who is he? what's his name?"

"Blamed if I know. Gone, you say? Got every derned red o' my money! Every derned red!"

"Don't you know anything at all about him?" I asked.

"Yes."

"What?"

"I know 'at he's the derndest, alfiredest, snatchin'est, best poker-player 'at ever dealt a card!"

"Is that all?"

"That's enough, I'd say. If you'd been beat out'n two hundred an' odd dollars you'd think you know'd a right smart, wouldn't ye?"

"Perhaps," said I. The question had a world of philosophy and logic in it.

The shattered wreck of a magnificent guitar lay in the middle of the floor. I picked it up, and, engraved on a heavy silver plate set in the ebony neck, I read the name, Georgina Olive Afton.

TROUT'S LUCK.

As early as eight o'clock the grand entrance gateway to the Kokomo fair ground was thronged with vehicles of almost every kind; horsemen, pedestrians, dogs and dust were borne forward together in clouds that boiled and swayed and tumbled. Noise seemed to be the chief purpose of every one and the one certain result of every thing in the crowd.

This had been advertised as the merriest day that might ever befall the quiet, honest folk of the rural regions circumjacent to Kokomo, and it is even hinted that aristocratic dames and business plethoric men of the town itself had caught somewhat of the excitement spread abroad by the announcement in the county papers, and by huge bills posted in conspicuous places, touching Le Papillon and his monster balloon, which balloon and which Le Papillon were pictured to the life, on the said posters, in the act of sailing over the sun, and under the picture, in remarkably distinct letters, "No humbug! go to the fair!"

Dozier's minstrel troupe was dancing and singing attendance on this agricultural exhibition, too, and somebody's whirling pavilion, a shooting gallery, a monkey show, the glass works, and what not of tempting promises of entertainments, "amusing and instructive."

Until eleven o'clock the entrance gateway to the fair ground was crowded. Farm wagons trundled in, drawn by sleek, well fed plough nags, and stowed full of smiling folk, old and young, male and female, from the out townships; buggies with youths and maidens, the sparkle of breastpins and flutter of ribbons; spring wagons full of students and hard bats from town; carriages brimming with laces, flounces, over skirts, fancy kid gloves, funny little hats and less bonnets, all fermented into languid ebullition by mild-eyed ladies; omnibuses that bore fleshy gentlemen, who wore linen dusters and silk hats and smoked fine cigars; and jammed in among all these were boys on skittish colts, old fellows on flea-bit gray mares, with now and then a reckless stripling on a mule. Occasionally a dog got kicked or run over, giving the assistance of his howls and yelps to the general din, and over all the dust hung heavily in a yellow cloud, shot through with the lightning of burnished trappings and echoing with the hoarse thunder of the trampling, shouting rumbling multitude. Indeed, that hot aguish autumn day let fall its sunshine on the heads and blew its feverish breath through the rifts of the greatest and liveliest mass of people ever assembled in Howard county.

Inside the extensive enclosure the multitude divided itself into streams, ponds, eddies, refluent currents and noisy whirlpools of people. Some rare attraction was everywhere.

Early in the day the eyes of certain of the rustic misses followed admiringly the forms of Jack Trout and Bill Powell, handsome young fellows dressed in homespun clothes, who, arm in arm, strolled leisurely across the grounds, looking sharply about for some proper place to begin the expenditure of what few dimes they had each been able to hoard up against this gala day. They had not long to hunt. On every hand the "hawkers hawked their wares."

Rising and falling, tender-toned, deftly managed, a voice rang out across the crowd pleading with those who had long desired a good investment for their money, and begging them to be sure and not let slip this last golden opportunity.

"Only a half a dollah! Come right along this way now! Here's the great golden scheme by which thousands have amassed untold fortunes! Here's your only and last chance to get two ounces of first class candy, with the probability of five dollars in gold coin, all for the small sum of half a dollah! And the cry is—still they come!"

The speaker was such a man as one often observes in a first class railway car, with a stout valise beside him containing samples, dressed with remarkable care, and ever on the alert to make one's acquaintance. He stood on top of a small table or tripod, holding in his hand a green pasteboard package just taken from a box at his feet.

"Only a half a dollah and a fortune in your grasp! Here's the gold! Roll right this way and run your pockets over!"

Drifting round with the tide of impulsive pleasure seekers into which they happened to fall, Jack Trout and Bill Powell floated past a bevy of lasses, the prettiest of whom was Minny Hart, a girl whose healthy, vivid beauty was fast luring Jack on to the rock of matrimonial proposals.

"Jimminy, but ain't she a little sweety!" exclaimed the latter, pinching Bill's arm as they passed, and glancing lovingly at Minny.

"You're tellin' the truth and talkin' it smooth," replied Bill, bowing to the girls with the swagger peculiar to a rustic who imagines he has turned a fine period. And with fluttering hearts the boys passed on.

"Roll on ye torrents! Only a half a dollah! Right this way if you want to become a bloated aristocrat in less than no time! Five dollahs in gold for only a half a dollah! And whose the next lucky man?"

Blown by the fickle, gusty breath of luck, our two young friends were finally wafted to the feet of this oily vendor of prize packages, and they there lodged, becalmed in breathless interest, to await their turn, each full of faith in the yellow star of his fortune—a gold coin of the value of five dollars. They stood attentively watching the results of other men's investments, feeling their fingers tingle when now and then some lucky fellow drew the coveted prize. Five dollars is a mighty temptation to a poor country boy in Indiana. That sum will buy oceans of fun at a fair where almost any "sight" is to be seen for the "small sum of twenty-five cents!"

Without stopping to take into consideration the possible, or rather, the probable result of such a venture, Bill Powell handed up his half dollar to the prize man, thus risking the major part of all the money he had, and stood trembling with excitement while the fellow broke open the chosen package. Was it significant of anything that a blue jay fluttered for a moment right over the crier's head just at the point of his detaching some glittering object from the contents of the box?

"Here you are, my friend; luck's a fortune!" yelled the man, as he held the gold coin high above his head, shaking it in full view of all eyes in the multitude. "Here you are! which 'd you rather have, the gold or five and a half in greenbacks?"

"Hand me in the rag chips—gold don't feel good to my fingers," answered Bill Powell, swaggering again and grasping the currency with a hand that shook with eagerness.

Jack Trout stood by, clutching in his feverish palm a two-dollar bill. His face was pale, his lips set, his muscles rigid. He hesitated to trust in the star of his destiny. He stood eyeing the bridge of Lodi, the dykes of Arcole. Would he risk all on a bold venture? His right shoulder began to twitch convulsively.

"Still it rolls, and who's the next lucky man? Don't all speak at once! Who wants five dollahs in gold and two ounces of delicious candy, all for the small sum of half a dollah?"

Jack made a mighty effort and passed up his two dollar bill.

"Bravely done; select your packages!" cried the vendor. Jack tremblingly pointed them out. Very carelessly and quietly the fellow opened them, and with a ludicrous grimace remarked—

"Eight ounces of mighty sweet candy, but nary a prize! Better luck next time! Only a half a dollah! And who's the next lucky man?"

A yell of laughter from the crowd greeted this occurrence, and Jack floated back on the recoiling waves of his chagrin till he was hidden in the dense concourse, and the uppermost thought in his mind found forcible expression in the three monosyllables: "Hang the luck!"

It is quite probable that of all the unfortunate adventurers that day singed in the yellow fire of that expert gambler's gold, Jack recognized himself as the most terribly burned. Putting his hands into his empty pockets, he sauntered dolefully about, scarcely able to look straight into the face of such friends as he chanced to meet. He acted as if hunting for something lost on the ground. Poor fellow, it was a real relief to him when some one treated him to a glass of lemonade, and, indeed, so much were his feelings relieved by the cool potation, that when, soon after, he met Minny Hart, he was actually smiling.

"O, Jack!" cried the pretty girl, "I'm so glad to see you just now, for I do want to go into the minstrel show *so bad!*" She shot a glance of coquettish tenderness right into Jack's heart. For a single moment he was blessed, but on feeling for his money and recalling the luckless result of his late venture, he felt a chill creep up his back, and a lump of the size of his fist jump up into his throat. Here was a bad affair for him. He stood for a single point of time staring into the face of his despair, then, acting on the only plan he could think of to escape from the predicament, he said:

"Wait a bit, Minny, I've got to go jist down here a piece to see a feller. I'll be back d'rectly. You stay right here and when I come back I'll trot you in."

So speaking, as if in a great hurry, and sweating cold drops, with a ghastly smile flickering on his face, the young man slipped away into the crowd.

Minny failed to notice his confusion, and so

called after him cheerily: "Well, hurry, Jack, for I'm most dead to see the show!"

What could Trout do? He spun round and round in that vast flood of people like a fish with but one eye. He rushed here, he darted there, and ever and anon, as a lost man returns upon his starting point, he came in sight of sweet Minny Hart patiently waiting for his return. Then he would spring back into the crowd like a deer leaping back into a thicket at sight of a hunter. Penniless at the fair, with Minny Hart waiting for him to take her into the show! Few persons can realize how keenly he now felt the loss of his money. He ought, no doubt, to have told the lass at once just how financial matters stood; but nothing was more remote from his mind than doing anything of the kind. He was too vain.

"Tell 'er I 'ain't got no money! No, sir-ee!" he muttered. "But what *am* I to do? Bust the luck! Hang the luck! Rot the luck!"

He hurried hither and thither, intent on nothing and taking no heed of the course he pursued. His cheeks were livid and his eyes had in them that painful, worried, wistful look so often seen in the eyes of men going home from ruin on Wall street.

Meantime that sea of persons surged this

way and that, flecked with a foam of ribbons and dancing bubbles of hats, now flowing slowly through the exhibition rooms a tide of critics, now breaking into groups and scattered throngs of babblers, anon uniting to roar round some novel engine suddenly set to work, or to break on the barrier of the trolling ring into a spray of cravats and a mist of flounces. Swimming round in this turbulent tide like a crazy flounder with but one fin, Jack finally found himself hard by the pavilion of the minstrels. He could hear somewhat of the side-splitting jokes, with the laughs that followed, the tinkle of banjo accompaniments and the mellow cadences of plantation songs, the rattle of castanets and the tattoo of the jig dancers' feet. A thirst like the thirst of fever took hold of him.

"Come straight along gentlemen and ladies! This celebrated troupe is now performing and twenty-five cents pays the bill! Only a quawtah of a dollah!" bawled the fat crier from his lofty perch. "That's right, my young man, take the young lady in! She's sure to love you better; walk right along!"

"Her lip am sweet as sugah,
Her eye am bright as wine,
Dat yaller little boogah
Her name am Emiline!"

sung by four fine voices, came bubbling from within. The music thrilled Jack to the bone, and he felt once more for his money. Not a cent. This was bad.

"You're the lad for me," continued the fat man on the high seat; "take your nice little sweetheart right in and let her see the fun. Walk right in!"

Jack looked to see who it was, and a pang shot through his heart and settled in the very marrow of his bones; for lo! arm in arm, Bill Powell and Minny Hart passed under the pavilion into the full glory of the show!

> "O cut me up for fish bait
>   An' feed me to de swine,
> Don't care where I goes to
>   So I has Emiline!"

sang the minstrel chorus.

"Dast him, he's got me!" muttered Jack as Bill and Minny disappeared within. He turned away, sick at heart, and this was far from the first throe of jealousy he had suffered on Bill's account. Indeed it had given him no little uneasiness lately to see how sweetly Minny sometimes smiled on young Powell.

"Yes, sir," Jack continued to mutter to himself, "yes, sir, he's got me! He's about three lengths ahead o' me, as these hoss fellers says, an' I don't know but what I'm distanced. Blow the blasted luck!"

Heartily tired of the fair, burning with rage, and jealousy, and despair, but still vaguely hoping against hope for some better luck from some visionary source, Jack strolled about, chewing the bitter cud of his feelings, his hands up to his elbows in his trowser pockets and his soul up to its ears in the flood of discontent. He puckered his mouth into whistling position, but it refused to whistle. He felt as if he had a corn cob crossways in his throat. The wind blew his new hat off and a mule kicked the top out of the crown.

"Only a half a dollah! Who's the next lucky man?" cried the prize package fellow. "I'm now going to sell a new sort of packages, each of which, beside the usual amount of choice candy, contains a piece of jewelry of pure gold! Who takes the first chance for only a half a dollah?"

"'Ere's your mule!" answered Bill Powell, as with Minny still clinging to his arm, he pushed through the crowd and handed up the money.

"Bravely done!" shouted the crier; "see what a beautiful locket and chain! Luck's a fortune! And who's the next to invest? Come right along and don't be afraid of a little risk! Only a half a dollah!"

Jack saw Bill put the glittering chain round Minny's neck and fasten the locket in her belt; saw the eyes of the sweet girl gleam proudly, gratefully; saw black spots dancing before his own eyes; saw Bill swagger and toss his head. He turned dizzily away, whispering savagely, "Dern 'im!"

Just here let me say that such an expression is not a profane one. I once saw a preacher kick at a little dog that got in his way on the sidewalk. The minister's foot missed the little dog and hit an iron fence, and the little dog bit the minister's other leg and jumped through the fence. The minister performed a *pas de zephyr* and very distinctly said "Dern 'im!" Wherefore I don't think it can be anything more than a mere puff of fretfulness.

After this Jack was for some time standing near the entrance to the "glass-works," a place where transparent steam engines and wonderful fountains were on exhibition. He felt a grim delight in tantalizing himself with looking at the pictures of these things and wishing he had money enough to pay the entrance fee. He saw persons pass in eagerly and come out calm and satisfied—men with their wives and children, young men with girls on their arms, prominent among whom were Bill and Minny, and one dapper sportsman even bought a ticket for his setter, and, patting the brute on the head, took him in.

"Onery nor a dog!" hissed Jack, shambling off, and once more taking a long deep dive under the surface of the crowd. A ground swell cast him again near the vender of prize packages.

"Only a half a dollah!" he yelled; "come where fortune smiles, and cares and poverty take flight, for only a half a dollah!"

"Jist fifty cents more'n I've got about my clothes!" replied Jack, and the bystanders, taking this for great wit, joined in a roar of laughter, while with a grim smile the desperate youth passed on till he found himself near the toe mark of a shooting gallery, where for five cents one might have two shots with an air gun. He stood there for a time watching a number of persons try their marksmanship. It was small joy to know that he was a fine off-hand shot, so long as he had not a nickel in his pocket, but still he stood there wishing he might try his hand.

"Cl'ar the track here! Let this 'ere lady

take a shoot!" cried a familiar voice; and a way was opened for Bill Powell and Minny Hart. The little maiden was placed at the toe mark and a gun given to her. She handled the weapon like one used to it. She raised it, shut one eye, took deliberate aim and fired.

"Centre!" roared the marker, as to the sound of a bell the funny little puppet leaped up and grinned above the target. Every body standing near laughed and some of the boys cheered vociferously. Minny looked sweeter than ever. Jack Trout felt famished. He begged a chew of tobacco of a stranger, and, grinding the weed furiously, walked off to where the yellow pavilion with its painted air-boats was whirling its cargoes of happy boys and girls round and round for the "Small sum of ten cents." A long, lean, red-headed fellow in one of the boats was paying for a ride of limitless length by scraping on a miserable fiddle. To Jack this seemed small labor for so much fun. How he envied the fiddler as he flew round, trailing his tunes behind him!

"Wo'erp there! Stop yer old merchine! We'll take a ride ef ye don't keer!"

The pavilion was stopped, a boat lowered for Bill Powell and Minny Hart, who got in side by side, and the fiddler struck up the tune of "Black-eyed Susie." Jack watched that happy couple go round and round, till, by the increased velocity, their two faces melted into one, which was neither Bill's nor Minny's—it was Luck's!

"He's got one outo me," muttered Jack; "I've got no money, can't fiddle for a ride, nor nothin', and I don't keer a ding what becomes o' me, nohow!"

With these words Jack wended his way to a remote part of the fair ground, where, under gay awnings, the sutlers had spread their tempting variety of cakes, pies, fruits, nuts and loaves. Here were persons of all ages and sizes—men, women and children—eating at well supplied tables. The sight was a fascinating one, and, though seeing others eat did not in the least appease his own hunger, Jack stood for a long time watching the departure of pies and the steady lessening of huge pyramids of sweet cakes. He particularly noticed one little table that had on its centre a huge peach pie, which table was yet unoccupied. While he was actually thinking over the plan of eating the pie and trusting to his legs to bear him beyond the reach of a dun, Bill and Minny sat down by the table and proceeded to discuss the delicious, red-hearted heap of pastry. At this point Bill caught Jack's eye:

"Come here, Jack," said he; "this pie's more'n we can eat, come and help us."

"Yes, come along, Jack," put in Minny in her sweetest way; "I want to tell you what a lot of fun we've had, and more than that, I want to know why you didn't come back and take me into the show!"

"I ain't hungry," muttered Jack, "and besides I've got to go see a feller."

He turned away almost choking.

"Bill's got me. 'Taint no use talkin', I'm played out for good. I'm a trumped Jack!"

He smiled a sort of flinty smile at his poor wit, and shuffled aimlessly along through the densest clots of the crowd.

And it so continued to happen, that wherever Jack happened to stop for any considerable length of time he was sure to see Bill and Minny enjoying some rare treat, or disappearing in or emerging from some place of amusement.

At last, driven to desperation, he determined on trying to borrow a dollar from his father. He immediately set about to find the old gentleman; a task of no little difficulty in such a crowd. It was Jack's forlorn hope, and it had a gloomy outlook; for old 'Squire Trout was thought by competent judges to be the stingiest man in the county. But hoping for the best, Jack hunted him here, there and everywhere, till at length he met a friend who said he had seen the 'Squire in the act of leaving the fair ground for home just a few minutes before.

Taking no heed of what folks might say, Jack, on receiving this intelligence, darted across the ground, out at the gate and down the road at a speed worthy of success; but alas! his hopes were doomed to wilt. At the first turn of the road he met a man who informed him that he had passed 'Squire Trout some three miles out on his way home, which home was full nine miles distant!

Panting, crestfallen, defeated, done for, poor Jack slowly plodded back to the fair ground gate, little dreaming of the new trouble that awaited him there.

"Ticket!" said a gruff voice as he was about to pass in. He recoiled, amazed at his own stupidity, as he recollected that he had not thought to get a check as he went out! He tried to explain, but it was no go.

"You needn't try that game on me," said the gatekeeper. "So just plank down your money or stay outside."

Then Jack got furious, but the gatekeeper

remarked that he had frequently "hearn it thunder afore this!"

Jack smiled like a corpse and turned away. Going a short distance down the road he climbed up and sat down on top of the fence of a late mown clover field. Then he took out his jack-knife and began to whittle a splinter plucked from a rail. His face was gloomy, his eyes lustreless. Finally he stretched himself, hungry, jealous, envious, hateful, on top of the fence with his head between the crossed stakes. His face thus upturned to heaven, he watched two crows drift over, high up in the torrid reaches of autumn air, hot as summer, even hotter, and allowed his lips free privilege to anathematize his luck. For a long time he lay thus, dimly conscious of the blue bird's song and the water-like ripple of the grass in the fence corners. "Minny, Minny Hart, Minny!" sang the meadow larks, and the burden of the grasshopper's ditty was—— "Only a half a dollah!"

All at once there arose from the fair ground a mighty chorus of yells, that went echoing off across the country to the bluffs of Wild-cat Creek and died far off in the woods toward Greentown. Jack did not raise his head, but lay there in a sort of morose stupor, knowing well that whatever the sport might be, he had no hand in it.

"Let 'em rip!" he muttered, "Bill's got me!"

Presently the wagons and other vehicles began to leave the ground, from one of which he caught the sound of a sweet, familiar voice. He looked just in time to get a glimpse of Mr. Hart's wagon, and in it, side by side, Bill Powell and Minny! A cloud of yellow dust soon hid them, and turning away his head, happening to glance upward, Jack saw, just disappearing in a thin white cloud, the golden disc of Le Papillon's balloon!

He immediately descended from his perch and began plodding his way home, muttering as he did so——

"Dast the luck! Ding the prize package feller! Doggone Bill Powell! Blame the old b'loon! Dern everybody!"

It was long after nightfall when he reached his father's gate. Hungry, weak, foot-sore, collapsed, he leaned his chin on the top rail of the gate and stood there for a moment while the starlight fell around him, sifted through the dusky foliage of the old beech trees, and from the far dim caverns of the night a voice smote on his ear, crying out tenderly, mockingly, persuasively——

"Only a half a dollah!"

And Jack slipped to his room and went supperless to bed, often during the night muttering, through the interstices of his sleep——
"Bill's got me!"

Big Medicine.

THE corner brick storehouse—in fact the only brick building in Jimtown—was to be sold at auction; and, consequently, by ten o'clock in the morning, a considerable body of men had collected near the somewhat dilapidated house, directly in front of which the auctioneer, a fat man from Indianapolis, mounted on an old goods box, began crying, partly through his tobacco-filled mouth and partly through his very unmusical nose, as follows:—

"Come up, gentlemen, and examine the new, beautiful and commodious property I now offer for sale! Walk round the house, men, and view it from every side. Go into it, if you like, up stairs and down, and then give me a bid, somebody, to start with. It is a very desirable house, indeed, gentlemen."

With this preliminary puff, the speaker paused and glanced slowly over his audience with the air of a practiced physiognomist.

The crowd before him was, in many respects, an interesting one. Its most prominent individual, and the hero of this sketch, was Dave Cook, sometimes called Dr. Cook, but more commonly answering to the somewhat savage sounding sobriquet of Big Medicine—a man some thirty-five years of age, standing six feet six in his ponderous boots; broad, bony, muscular, a real giant, with a strongly marked Roman face, and brown, shaggy hair. He was dressed in a soiled and somewhat patched suit of butternut jeans, topped off with a wide rimmed wool hat, wonderfully battered, and lopped in every conceivable way. He wore a watch, the chain of which, depending from the waistband of his pants, was of iron, and would have weighed fully a pound avoirdupois. He stood quite still, near the auctioneer, smoking a clay pipe, his herculean arms folded on his breast, his feet far apart. As for the others of the crowd, they were, taken collectively, about such as one used always to see in the "dark corners" of Indiana, such as Boone county used to be before the building of any railroads through it, such as the particular locality of Jimtown was before the ditching law and the I. B. & W. Railway had lifted the fog and enlightened the miasmatic swamps and densely timbered bog lands of that region of elms, burr oaks, frogs and herons. Big Medicine seemed to be the only utterly complacent man in the assembly. All the others discovered evidences of much inward disturbance, muttering mysteriously to each other, and casting curious, inquiring glances at an individual, a stranger in the place, who, with a pair of queer green spectacles astride his nose, and his arms crossed behind him, was slowly sauntering about the building offered for sale, apparently examining it with some care. His general appearance was that of a well dressed gentleman, which of itself was enough to excite remark in Jimtown, especially when an auction was on hand, and everybody felt jolly.

"Them specs sticks to that nose o' his'n like a squir'l to a knot!" said one.

"His pantaloons is ruther inclined to be knock-kneed," put in an old, grimy sinner leaning on a single barrelled shot gun.

"Got lard enough onto his hair to shorten a mess o' pie crust," added a liver colored boy.

"Walks like he'd swallered a fence rail, too," chimed in a humpbacked fellow split almost to his chin.

"Chaws mighty fine terbacker, you bet."

"Them there boots o' his'n set goin' an' comin' like a grubbin' hoe onto a crooked han'le."

"Well, take 'm up one side and down t'other, he's a mod'rately onery lookin' feller."

These remarks were reckoned smart by those who perpetrated them, and were by no means meant for real slurs on the individual at whom they were pointed. Indeed they were delivered in guarded undertones, so that he might not hear them; and he, meanwhile, utterly ignorant of affording any sport, continued his examination of the house, the while some happy frogs in a neighboring pond rolled out a rattling, jubilant chorus, and the summer wind poured through the leafy tops of the tall elms and athletic burr oaks with a swash and roar like a turbulent river.

"What am I now offered for this magnificent property? Come, give me a bid! Speak up lively! What do I hear for the house?"

The auctioneer, as he spoke, let his eyes wander up the walls of the old, dingy building, to where the blue birds and the peewees had built in the cracks and along the warped cornice and broken window frames, and just then it chanced that a woman's face appeared at one of those staring holes, which, with broken lattice and shattered glass, still might be called a window. The face was a plump, cheerful one, the more radiant from contrast with the dull wall around it—a face one could never forget, however, and would recall often, if for nothing but the fine fall of yellow hair that framed it in. It was a sweet, winning, intellectual face, full of the gentlest womanly charms.

"Forty dollars for the house, 'oman and all!" cried Big Medicine, gazing up at the window in which, for the merest moment, the face appeared.

The man with the green spectacles darted a quick glance at the speaker.

"I am bid forty dollars, gentlemen, forty dollars, do all hear? Agoing for forty dollars! Who says fifty?" bawled the auctioneer.

The crowd now swayed earnestly forward, closing in solid order around the goods box. Many whiskered, uncouth, but not unkindly faces were upturned to the window only in time to see the beautiful woman disappear quite hastily.

"Hooray for the gal!" cried a lusty youth, whose pale blue eyes made no show of contrast with his faded hair and aguish complexion. "Dad, can't ye bid agin the doctor so as I kin claim 'er?"

"Fifty dollars!" shouted the sunburnt man addressed as Dad.

This made the crowd lively. Every man nudged his neighbor, and the aguish, blue-eyed boy grinned in a ghastly, self-satisfied way.

"Agoing at fifty dollars! Fiddlesticks! The house is worth four thousand. No fooling here now! Agoing at only fifty dollars—going—"

"Six hundred dollars," said he of the green glasses in a clear, pleasant voice.

"Six hundred dollars!" echoed the auctioneer in a triumphant thunderous tone. "That sounds like business. Who says the other hundred?"

"Hooray for hooray, and hooray for hooray's daddy!" shouted the tallow-faced lad.

The frogs pitched their song an octave higher, the blue birds and peewees wheeled through the falling floods of yellow sunlight, and lower and sweeter rose the murmur of the tide of pulsating air as it lifted and swayed the fresh sprays of the oaks and elms. The well dressed stranger lighted a cigar, took off his green glasses and put them carefully in his pocket, then took a cool straight look at Big Medicine.

The Roman face of the latter was just then

a most interesting one. It was expressive of more than words could rightly convey. Six hundred dollars, cash down, was a big sum for the crazy old house, but he had made up his mind to buy it, and now he seemed likely to have to let it go or pay more than it was worth. The stem of his clay pipe settled back full three inches into his firmly-set mouth, so that there seemed imminent danger to the huge brown moustache that overhung the fiery bowl. He returned the stare of the stranger with interest, and said—

"Six hundred an' ten dollars."

"Agoing, a——," began the auctioneer.

"Six twenty," said the stranger.

"Ago——."

"Six twenty-one!" growled Big Medicine.

"Six twenty-five!" quickly added his antagonist.

Big Medicine glanced heavenward, and for a moment allowed his eyes to follow the flight of a great blue heron that slowly winged its way, high up in the yellow summer reaches of splendor, toward the distant swamps where the white sycamores spread their fanciful arms above the dark green maples and dusky witch-hazel thickets. The auctioneer, a close observer, saw an ashy hue, a barely discernible shade, ripple across the great Roman face as Big Medicine said, in a jerking tone:

"Six twenty-five and a half!"

The stranger took his cigar from his mouth and smiled placidly. No more imperturbable countenance could be imagined.

"Six twenty-six!" he said gently.

"Take the ole house an' be derned to you!" cried Big Medicine, looking furiously at his antagonist. "Take the blamed ole shackemerack an' all the cussed blue-birds an' peerweers to boot, for all I keer!"

Everybody laughed, and the auctioneer continued:

"Agoing for six twenty-six! Who says seven hundred? Bid up lively! Agoing once, agoing twice—once, twice, three-e-e-e-e times! Sold to Abner Golding for six hundred and twenty-six dollars, and as cheap as dirt itself!"

"Hooray for the man who hed the most money!" shouted the tallow-faced boy.

The sale was at an end. The auctioneer came down from his box and wiped his face with a red handkerchief. The crowd, as if blown apart by a puff of wind, scattered this way and that, drifting into small, grotesque groups to converse together on whatever topic might happen to suggest itself. Big Medicine seemed inclined to be alone, but the irrepressible youth of the saffron skin ambled up to him and said, in a tone intended for comic:

"Golly, doctor, but didn't that 'ere gal projuce a orful demand for the ole house! Didn't she set the ole trap off when she peeked out'n the winder!"

Big Medicine looked down at the strapping boy, much as a lion might look at a field rat or a weasel, then he doubled his hand into an enormous fist and held it under the youth's nose, saying in a sort of growl as he did so:

"You see this 'ere bundle o' bones, don't ye?"

"Guess so," replied the youth.

"Well, would you like a small mess of it?"

"Not as anybody knows of."

"Well, then, keep yer derned mouth shet!"

Which, accordingly, the boy proceeded to do, ambling off as quickly as possible.

About this time, the stranger, having put the green spectacles back upon his nose, walked in the direction of 'Squire Tadmore's office, accompanied by the young woman who had looked from the window. When Big Medicine saw them he picked up a stick and began furiously to whittle it with his jack-knife. His face wore a comically mingled look of chagrin, wonder, and something like a new and thrilling delight. He puffed out great volumes of smoke, making his pipe wheeze audibly under the vigor of his draughts. He was certainly excited.

"Orful joke the boys 'll have on me arter this," he muttered to himself. "Wonder if the 'oman's the feller's wife? Monstrous poorty, shore's yer born!"

He soon whittled up one stick. He immediately dived for another, this time getting hold of a walnut knot. A tough thing to whittle, but he attacked it as if it had been a bit of white pine. Soon after this 'Squire Tadmore's little boy came running down from his father's office to where Big Medicine stood.

"Mr. Big Medicine," cried he, all out of breath, "that 'ere man what bought the ole house wants to see you partic'ler!"

"Mischief he does! Tell 'im to go to——; no, wait a bit. Guess I'll go tell 'im myself."

And, so saying, he moved at a slashing pace down to the door of the 'Squire's office. He thrust his great hirsute head inside the room, and glaring at the mild mannered stranger, said:

"D'ye want to see me?"

Mr. Golding got up from his seat and coming out took Big Medicine familiarly by the arm, meanwhile smiling in the most friendly way.

"Come one side a little, I wish to speak with you privately, confidentially."

Big Medicine went rather sulkily along. When they had gone some distance from the house Mr. Golding lifted his spectacles from his nose, and turning his calm, smiling eyes full upon those of Big Medicine, said, with a shrug of his finely cut shoulders:

"I outbid you a little, my friend, but I'm blessed if I haven't got myself into a ridiculous scrape on account of it."

"How so?" growled Big Medicine.

"Why, when I come to count my funds I'm short a half dollar."

"You're what?"

"I lack just a half dollar of having enough money to pay for the house, and I thought I'd rather ask you to loan me the money than anybody else here."

Big Medicine stood for a time in silence, whittling away, as if for dear life, on the curly knot. Dreamy gusts of perfumed heat swept by from adjacent clover and wheat fields, where the blooms hung thick; little whirlwinds played in the dust at their feet as little whirlwinds always do in summer; and far away, faint, and made tenderly musical by distance, were heard the notes of a country dinner-horn. Big Medicine's ample chest swelled, and swelled, and then he burst at the mouth with a mighty bass laugh, that went battling and echoing round the place. Mr. Golding laughed too, in his own quiet, gentlemanly way. They looked at each other and laughed, then looked off toward the swamps and laughed. Big Medicine put his hands in his pockets almost up to the elbows, and leaned back and laughed out of one corner of his mouth while holding his pipe in the other.

"I say, mister," said he at length, "a'n't you railly got but six hundred and twenty-five an' a half?"

"Just that much to a cent, and no more," replied Mr. Golding, with a comical smile and bow.

Big Medicine took his pipe from his mouth, gave the walnut knot he had dropped a little kick and guffawed louder and longer than before. To have been off at a little distance watching them would have convinced any one that Mr. Golding was telling some rare anecdote, and that Big Medicine was convulsed with mirth, listening.

"Well I'm derned if 'taint quare," cried the

latter, wringing himself into all sorts of grotesque attitudes in the ecstasy of his amusement. "You outbid me half a dollar and then didn't have the half a dollar neither! Wha, wha, wha-ee!" and his cachinnations sounded like rolling of moderate thunder.

At the end of this he took out a greasy wallet and paid Mr. Golding the required amount in silver coin. His chagrin had vanished before the stranger's quiet way of making friends.

A week passed over Jimtown. A week of as rare June weather as ever lingered about the cool places of the woods, or glimmered over the sweet clover fields all red with a blush of bloom, where the field larks twittered and the buntings chirped, and where the laden bees rose heavily to seek their wild homes in the hollows of the forests. By this time it was generally known in Jimtown that Mr. Golding would soon receive a stock of goods with which to open a "store" in the old corner brick; but Big Medicine knew more than any of his neighbors, for he and Golding had formed a partnership to do business under the "name and style" of Cook & Golding.

This Abner Golding had lately been a wealthy retail man in Cincinnati, and had lost everything by the sudden suspension of a bank wherein the bulk of his fortune was on deposit. His creditors had made a run on him and he had been able to save just the merest remnant of his goods, and a few hundred dollars in money. Thus he came to Jimtown to begin life and business anew.

To Big Medicine the week had been a long one; why, it would not be easy to tell. No doubt there had come a turning point in his life. In those days, and in that particular region, to be a 'store keeper' was no small honor. But Big Medicine acted strangely. He wandered about, with his hands in his pockets, whistling plaintive tunes, and often he was seen standing out before the old corner brick, gazing up at one of the vacant windows where pieces of broken lattice were swaying in the wind. At such times he muttered softly to himself:

"Ther's wher I fust seed the gal."

Four big road wagons (loaded with boxes), three of them containing the merchandise and one the scanty household furniture of Mr. Golding and his daughter Carrie, came rumbling into Jimtown. Big Medicine was on hand, a perfect Hercules at unloading and unpacking. Mr. Golding was sadly pleasant; Carrie was roguishly observant, but womanly and quiet.

The tallow-faced youth and two or three others stood by watching the proceedings. The former occasionally made a remark at which the others never failed to laugh.

"Ef ye'll notice, now," said he, "it's a fac 'at whenever Big Medicine goes to make a big surge to lift a box, he fust takes a peep at the gal, an' that 'ere seems to kinder make 'im 'wax strong an' multiply,' as the preacher says, an' then over goes the box!"

"Has a awful effect on his narves," some one replied.

"I'm a thinkin'," added tallow-face, "'at ef Big Medicine happens to look at the gal about the time he goes to make a trade, it 'll have sich a power on 'im 'at he'll sell a yard o' caliker for nigh onto forty dollars!"

"Er a blanket overcoat for 'bout twelve an' a half cents!" put in another.

"I'm kinder weakly," resumed tallow-face with a comical leer at Big Medicine; "wonder if 't wouldn't be kinder strengthnin' on me ef I'd kinder sidle up towards the gal myself?"

"I'll sidle up to you!" growled Big Medicine; and making two strides of near ten feet each, he took the youth by his faded flaxen hair, and holding him clear of the ground, administered a half dozen or so of resounding kicks, then tossed him to one side, where he fell in a heap on the ground. When he got on his feet again he began to bristle up and show fight, but when Big Medicine reached for him he ambled off.

In due time the goods were all placed on the shelves and Mr. Golding's household furniture arranged in the upper rooms where he purposed living, Carrie acting as housekeeper.

On the first evening after all things had been put to rights, Mr. Golding said to Big Medicine:

"I suppose we ought to advertise."

"Do how?"

"Advertise."

"Sartinly," said Big Medicine, having not the faintest idea of what his partner meant.

"Who can we get to paint our fence advertisements?"

A gleam of intelligence shot from Big Medicine's eyes. He knew now what was wanted. He remembered once, on a visit to Crawfordsville, seeing these fence advertisements. He comprehended in a moment.

"O, I know what ye mean, now," he said, with a grin, as if communing with himself on some novel suggestion. "I guess I kin 'tend to that my own self. The moon shines to-night, don't it?"

"Yes; why?"

"I'll do the paintin' to-night. A good ijée has jist struck me. You jist leave it all to me."

So the thing was settled, and Big Medicine was gone all night.

The next day was a sluice of rain. It poured incessantly from daylight till dark. Big Medicine sat on the counter in the corner brick and chuckled. His thoughts were evidently very pleasant ones. Mr. Golding was busy marking goods and Carrie was helping him. The great grey eyes of Big Medicine followed the winsome girl all the time. When night came, and she went up stairs, he said to Golding:

"That gal o' your'n is a mighty smart little 'oman."

"Yes, and she's all I have left," replied Mr. Golding in a sad tone.

Big Medicine stroked his brown beard, whistled a few turns of a jig tune, and, jumping down from the counter, went out into the drizzly night. A few rods from the house he turned and looked up at the window. A little form was just vanishing from it.

"Ther's wher I fust seed the gal," he murmured, then turned and went his way, occupied with strange, sweet imaginings. As a matter of the merest conjecture, it is interesting to dwell upon the probable turn taken by his thoughts as he slowly stalked through the darkness and rain that night; but I shall not trench on what, knowing all that I do, seems sanctified and hallowed. It would be breaking a sacred confidence. Who has stood and watched for a form at a window? Who has expressed, in language more refined, to the inner fountain of human sympathy, the idea conveyed in the rough fellow's remark? Who that has, let him recall the time and the place holy in his memory.

"Ther's wher I fust seed the gal," said the man, and went away to his lonely bed to dream the old new dream. All night the rain fell, making rich music on the roof and pouring through his healthy slumber a sound like the flowing of strange rivers in a land of new delights—a land into which he had strayed hand in hand with some one, the merest touch of whose hand was rapture, the simplest utterance of whose voice was charming beyond expression. The old new dream. The dream of flesh that is divine—the vision of blood that is love's wine—the apocalypse that bewildered the eyes of the old singer when from a flower of foam in the sweet green sea rose the Cytherean Venus. We have all dreamed the dream and found it sweet.

It is quite probable that no fence advertisements ever paid as well, or stirred up as big a "muss" as those painted by Big Medicine on the night mentioned heretofore. As an artist our Hoosier was not a genius, but he certainly understood how to manufacture a notoriety. If space permitted I would copy all those rude notices for your inspection; but I must be content with a few random specimens taken from memory, with an eye to brevity. They are characteristic of the man and in somewhat an index of the then state of society in and around Jimtown. On Deacon Jones's fence was scrawled the following: "Dern yer ole sole, ef yer want good Koffy go to Cook & Golding's nu stoar."

John Butler, a nice old quaker, had the following daubed on his gate: "Yu thievin' duk-legged ya and na ole cuss, ef the sperit muves ye, go git a broad-brimmed straw hat at Cook & Golding's great stand at Jimtown." The side of William Smith's pig pen bore this: "Bill, ye ornery sucker, come traid with Cook & Golding at the ole corner brick in Jimtown." Old Peter Gurley found writing to the following effect on his new wagon bed: "Ef yoor dri or anything, you'll find a virtoous Kag of ri licker at Cook & Golding's." On a large plank nailed to a tree at Canaan's Cross Roads all passers by saw the following: "Git up an brindle! Here's yer ole and faithful mewl! Come in gals and git yer dofunny tricks and fixens, hats, caps, bonnets, parrysols, silk petty-coat-sleeves and other injucements too noomerous too menshen! Rip in—we're on it! Call at Cook & Golding's great corner brick!"

These are fair specimens of what appeared everywhere. How one man could have done so much in one night remains a mystery. Some people swore, some threatened to prosecute, but finally everybody went to the corner brick to trade. Jimtown became famous on account of Big Medicine and the corner brick store.

The sun rose through the morning gate beyond the quagmires east of Jimtown and set through the evening gate past the ponds and maple swamps to the west. The winds blew and there were days of calm. The weather ran through its mutations of heat and cold. The herons flew over, the blue birds twittered and went away and came again, and the peewees disappeared and returned. A whole year had rolled round and it was June again, with the air full of rumors about the building of a railroad through Jimtown.

During this flow of time Big Medicine had feasted his eyes on the bright curls and brighter eyes of Carrie Golding, till his heart had become tender and happy as a child's. They rarely conversed more than for him to say, "Miss Carrie, look there," or for her to call out, "Please, Mr. Cook, hand me down this bolt of muslin." But Big Medicine was content.

It was June the 8th, about ten o'clock in the morning, and Big Medicine was slowly making his way from his comfortable bachelor's cabin to the corner brick. A peculiar smile was on his face, his heart was fluttering strangely, and all on account of a little circumstance of the preceding day, now fresh in his memory. Great boy that he was, he was poring over a single sweet smile Carrie Golding had given him!

The mail hack stood at the post-office door, whence Mr. Golding was coming with a letter in his hand. Big Medicine stopped and looked up at the window. There stood Carrie. She was looking hopefully toward her father. Big Medicine smiled and murmured:

"Ther's wher I fust seed the gal—bless her sweet soul!" There was a whole world of sincere happiness in the tones of his voice.

Mr. Golding passed him hastily, his green spectacles on his nose, and a great excitement flashing from his face. Big Medicine gazed wonderingly after his partner till he saw him run up stairs to Carrie's room. Then he thought he heard Carrie cry out joyfully, but it may have been the wind.

When an hour had passed Mr. Golding and Carrie came down dressed for travelling. How strangely, wondrously beautiful the girl now looked! Mr. Golding was as nervous as an old woman. He rubbed his thin white hands together rapidly and said:

"Mr. Cook, I have glorious news this morning!"

"And what mought it be?" asked Big Medicine, as a damp chilliness crept over him, and his face grew pinched and almost as white as his shirt bosom.

"Krofton & Kelly, the bankers, have resumed payment, and I'll get all my money! It *is* glorious news, is it not, my friend?"

Big Medicine was silent. He tried to speak, but his mouth was dry and powerless. A mist drifted across his eyes. He hardly realized where he was or what was said, but he knew all.

"I have concluded to give you this house and

all my interest in this store. You must not refuse. I haven't time to make the transfer now, but I'll not neglect it. Carrie and I must hasten at once to Cincinnati. The hack is waiting; so good bye, my dear friend, God bless you!" Mr. Golding wrung his partner's cold, limp hand, without noticing how fearfully haggard that Roman face had suddenly grown.

"Good bye, Mr. Cook," said Carrie in her sweet, sincere way. "I'm real sorry to leave you and the dear old house—but—but—good bye, Mr. Cook. Come to see us in Cincinnati. Good bye." She gave him her hand also.

He smiled a wan, flickering smile, like the last flare of a fire whose fuel is exhausted. Carrie's woman's heart sank under that look, though she knew not wherefore.

The hack passed round the curve of the road.

They were gone!

Big Medicine stood alone in the door of the corner brick. He looked back over his shoulders at the well filled shelves and muttered:

"She ain't here, and what do I want of the derned old store?"

The wind rustled the elm leaves and tossed the brown locks of the man over his great forehead; the blue birds sang on the roof; the dust rose in little columns along the street; and, high over head, in the yellow mist of the fine June weather, sailed a great blue heron, going to the lakes. Big Medicine felt like one deserted in the wilderness. He stood there a while, then closed and locked the door and went into the woods. A month passed before he returned. Jimtown wondered and wondered. But when he did return his neighbors could not get a word out of him. He was silent, moody, listless. Where had he been? Only hunting for Mr. Golding and Carrie. He found them, after a long search, in a splendid residence on the heights just out of Cincinnati. Mr. Golding greeted him cordially, but somehow Big Medicine felt as though he were shaking hands with some one over an insurmountable barrier. That was not the Mr. Golding he had known.

"Carrie is out in the garden. She will be glad to see you. Go along the hall there. You will see the gate."

Mr. Golding waved his hand after the manner of a very rich man, and a patronizing tone would creep into his voice. Somehow Big Medicine looked terribly uncouth.

With a hesitating step and a heart full of unreal sensations, Big Medicine opened the little gate and strode into the flower garden. Suddenly a vision, such as his fancy had never pictured, burst on his dazzled eyes. Flowers and vines and statues and fountains; on every hand rich colors; perfumes so mixed and intensified that his senses almost gave way; long winding walks; fairy-like bowers and music. He paused and listened. A heavy voice, rich and manly, singing a ballad—some popular love song—to the sweet accompaniment of a violin, and blended through it all, like a silvery thread, the low sweet voice of Carrie Golding. The poor fellow held his breath till the song was done.

Two steps forward and Big Medicine towered above the lovers.

Carrie sprang to her feet with a startled cry; then, recognizing the intruder, she held out her little hand and welcomed him. Turning to her lover she said:

"Henry, this is Mr. Cook, lately papa's partner in Indiana."

The lover was a true gentleman, so he took the big hard hand of the visitor and said he was glad to see him.

Big Medicine stood for a few moments holding a hand of each of the lovers. Presently a tremor took possession of his burly frame. He did not speak a word. His breast swelled and his face grew awfully white. He put Carrie's hand in that of her lover and turned away. As he did so a tear, a great bitter drop, rolled down his haggard cheek. A few long strides and Big Medicine was gone.

Shrilly piped the blue birds, plaintively sang the peewees, sweetly through the elms and burr oaks by the corner brick blew the fresh summer wind, as, just at sunset, Big Medicine once more stood in front of the old building with his eyes fixed on the vacant, staring window.

It was scarcely a minute that he stood there, but long enough for a tender outline of the circumstances of the past year to rise in his memory.

A rustling at the broken lattice, a sudden thrill through the iron frame of the watching man, a glimpse of a sweet face—no, it was only a fancy. The house was still, and old and desolate. It stared at him like a death's head.

Big Medicine raised his eyes toward heaven, which was now golden and flashing resplendently with sunset glories. High up, as if almost touching the calm sky, a great blue heron was toiling heavily westward. Taking the course chosen by the lone bird, Big Medicine went away, and the places that knew him once know him no more forever.

THE VENUS OF BALHINCH.

WHEN I returned from Europe with a finished education, I found that my fortune also was finished in the most approved modern style, so I left New York and drifted westward in search of employment. At length I came to Indiana, and, having not even a cent left, and mustering but one presentable suit of clothes, I looked about me in a hungry, half desperate sort of way, till I pounced upon the school in Balhinch. Now Balhinch is not a town, nor a cross-road place, nor a post-office —it is simply a neighborhood in the southwestern corner of Union Township, Montgomery County—a neighborhood *sui generis*, stowed away in the breaks of Sugar Creek, containing as good, quiet, law-abiding folk as can be found anywhere outside of Switzerland. My school was a small one in numbers, but the pupils ranged from four to six feet three in altitude, and well proportioned. The most advanced class had thumbed along pretty well through the spelling book. I need not take up your time with the school, however, for it has nothing at all to do with my story, excepting merely to explain how I came to be in Balhinch, in the State of Indiana.

My first sight of Susie Adair was on Sunday at the Methodist prayer meeting. I was sitting with my back to a window and facing the door of the log meeting house when she entered. It was July—a hot glary day, but a steady wind blew cool and sweet from the southwest, bringing in all sorts of woodland odors. The grasshoppers were chirruping in the little timothy field hard by, and over in a bit of woodland pasture a swarm of blue jays were worrying a crow, keeping up an incessant squeaking and chattering. The dumpy little class leader—the only little man in Balhinch—had just begun to give out the hymn

"Love is the sweetest bud that blows,
Its beauties never die,
On earth among the saints it grows
And ripens in the sky," &c.,

when Susie came in. Ben Crane was sitting by me. He nudged me with his elbow and whispered:

"How's that 'ere for poorty?"

I made him no answer, but remained staring

at the girl till long after she had taken her seat. Nature plays strange tricks. Susie, the daughter of farmer Adair, was as beautiful in the face as any angel could be, and her form was as perfect as that of the Cnidian Venus. Her motion when she walked was music, and as she sat in statuesque repose, the undulations of her queenly form were those of perfect ease, grace and strength. Her hands were small and taper, a little browned from exposure, as was also her face. Her hair was the real classic gold, and her grey eyes were riant with health and content. When her red lips parted to sing, they discovered small even teeth, as white as ivory. I can give you no idea of her. Physically she was perfection's self in the mould of a Venus of the grandest type. Her head, too, was an intellectual one (though feminine), in the best sense of the word. The first thought that flashed across my mind was embodied in the words—*A Venus*—and I still think of her as the best model I ever saw.

"How's that for poorty?" repeated Crane.

"Who is she?" I replied interrogatively.

"She's my jewlarker," said he.

"Your what?"

"My sweetheart."

"What is her name?"

"Susie Adair."

So I came to know her and admire her, and even before that little prayer meeting was over I loved her. Introductions were an unknown institution in Balhinch, but I was not long in finding a way to the personal acquaintance of Susie. I found her remarkably intelligent for one of her limited opportunities, very fond of reading, sprightly in conversation, womanly, modest, sweet tempered, and, indeed, altogether charming as well as superbly beautiful.

As for me, I am an insignificant looking man, and then I was even more so than now. My hair is terribly stiff and red, you know, and my eyes are very pale blue, nearly white. My neck is very long and has a large Adam's apple. I am small and narrow chested, and have slender bow legs. My teeth are uneven and my nose is pug. I have a very fine thin voice, decidedly nasal, as you perceive. One thing, however, I am well educated, polite, and not a bad conversationalist.

Susie was a most entertaining and perplexing study for me from the start. She treated me with decided consideration and kindness, seemed deeply interested in my accounts of my travels, asked me many questions about the old world and good society, sat for hours at a time listening to me as I read aloud. In fact I felt that I was impressing her deeply, but she would go with Ben Crane, that long, awkward, ignorant gawk. How could a young woman of such fine magnetic presence, and endowed with such genuine, instinctive purity of taste in everything else, bear the presence of a rough greenhorn like that? Finally I said to myself: she is kind and good; she cannot bear to slight Ben, though she cares nothing for him.

What a strange state being in love is! It is like dreaming in the grass. One hears the flow of the wind—it is the breath of love—one smells the flowers, and it is the perfume of a young cheek, the sharp fragrance of blonde curls. What dreams I had in those days! I could scarcely endure my school to the end of the first three months. Then I gave it up, and collecting my wages purchased me some fine clothes—that is, fine for the time and the place. I recollect that suit now, and wonder how a man of my taste could have borne to wear it. A black coat, a scarlet vest and white pants, ending with calf boots and a very tall silk hat! If you should see me dressed that way now you would laugh till your ribs would hurt. I do not know how true it is, but, from a pretty good source, I heard that Ben Crane said I looked like a red-headed woodpecker. One thing I do know, I never saw a woodpecker with a freckled face. I have a freckled face.

Ben soon recognized me as his rival and treated me with supreme impertinence, even going so far as to rub his fist under my nose and swear at me—a thing at which I felt profoundly indignant, and considering which I was surely justified in sticking a lucifer match into Ben's six valuable hay stacks one night thereafter. It was a great fire, and two hundred dollars loss to Ben. Let him keep his fist out from under my nose.

But I must come to my story, cutting short these preliminaries. It is a story I never tire of telling, and a story which has elicited ejaculations from many.

It was a ripe sweet day in the latter part of September—clear, but hazy and dreamful—a prelude to the Indian summer. I stood before the glass in my room at 'Squire Jones's, where I boarded, and very carefully arranged my bright blue neck-tie. Then I combed my hair. I never have got thoroughly familiar with my hair. I cannot, even now, comb it, while looking in a glass, without cringing for fear of burning my fingers. The long, wavy red locks flow through the comb like flames, and underneath is a gleam of live coals and red hot ashes. Ben Crane said he believed my head had set his hay stacks a-fire. Maybe it did. I wished that a stray flash from the same source would kindle the heart of Susie Adair and heat it until it lay under her Cytherean breasts a puddle of molten love. I put my silk hat carefully upon my head and wriggled my hands into a pair of kid gloves; then, walking-stick in hand, I set out to know my fate at the hands of Susie. My way was across a stubble field in which the young clover, sown in the spring, displayed itself in a variety of fantastic modes. Have you ever noticed how much grass is like water? Some one, Hawthorne, perhaps, has spoken of "a gush of violets," and Swinburne, going into one of his musical frenzies, cries:

> "Where tides of grass break into foam of flowers."

I have seen pools of clover and streams of timothy; I have stood ankle deep in shoal blue grass and have watched for hours the liquid ripples of the red top. I have seen the field sparrows dive into the green waves of young wheat, and the black starlings wade about in the sink-foil of southern countries.

Grass is a liquid that washes earth's face till it shines like that of a clean, healthy child. But clover prefers to stand in pools and eddies, in which oft and oft I have seen the breasts of meadow larks shine like gold, the while a few sweet notes, like rung silver, rose and trembled above the trefoil, all woven, in and out, through the swash of the wind's palpitant currents—a music of unspeakable influence. Swallows skim the surface of grass just as they do that of water. When the summer air agitates the smooth bosom of a broad green meadow field, you will see these little random arrows glancing along the emerald surface, cutting with barbed wings through the tossing, bloom-capped waves, thence ricochetting high into the bright air to whirl and fall again as swiftly as before. Many a time I have traced streams of grass to their fresh fountains, where jets of tender foliage and bubbles of tinted flowers welled up from dark, rich earth, and flowed away, with a velvet rustle and a ripple like blown floss, to break and recoil and eddy against the dark shadows of a distant grove. Such a fountain is a place of fragrance and joy. The bees go thither to get the sweetest honey, and find it a very Hybla. The butterflies float about it in a dreamful trance, while in the cool, damp shade of a dock leaf squats a great toad, like a slimy dragon guarding the gate of a paradise.

As I slowly walked across that stubble field, now and then stepping into a tuft of clover, out from which a quail would start, whirling away in a convulsion of flight, I allowed dreams of bliss to steal rosily across my brain. I scarcely saw the great gold-sharded beetles that hummed and glanced in the mellow sunlight. I heard like one half asleep, as if far away, the sharp twitter of the blue bird and the tender piping of the meadow lark. Susie Adair was all my thought. I recollect that, just as I climbed the fence at the farther side of the clover field, I saw a white winged, red headed woodpecker pounce upon and carry off a starry opal-tinted butterfly, and I thought how sweet it would be if I could thus steal away into the free regions of space the object of my gentler passion. But then what wonderful big wings I should have needed, for my Venus of the hollow of the hill of Balhinch was no airy thing. Her tall, strong body and magnificent limbs equalled one hundred and forty pounds avoirdupois! My own weight was about one hundred and twenty.

As I neared Susie's home I began, for the

first time in my life, to suffer from palpitation. The shadow of a doubt floated in the autumn sun-light. I set my teeth together and resolved not to be faint hearted. I must go in boldly and plead my cause and win.

When I reached the gate of the Adair farmhouse I had to look straight over the head of a very large, sanctimonious-faced bull-dog to get a view of the vine covered porch. This dog looked up at me and smiled ineffably; then he came to the gate and stood over against me, peeping between the slats. I hesitated. About this time Ben Crane came out of the house with a banjo in his hand. He had been playing for Susie. He was a natural musician.

"'Feared o' the dog, Mr. Woodpecker?" said he. "Begone, Bull!" and he kicked the big-headed canine aside so that I could go in.

I heard him thrumming on his banjo far down the road as Susie met me at the door. How wondrously beautiful she was!

"Sit down Mr. ———, and, if you do not care, I'll bring the churn in and finish getting the butter while we talk."

I was delighted—I was charmed—fascinated. Susie's father had gone to a distant village, and her mother, a gentle work-worn matron, was in the other room spinning flax, humming, meantime, snatches of camp meeting hymns. The sound of that spinning-wheel seemed to me strangely mournful and sad, but Susie's deep, clear gray eyes and cheerful voice were the very soul of joyousness, health and youth. She brought in a great fragrant cedar churn, made to hold six or eight gallons of cream, and forthwith began her labor. She stood as she worked, and the exercise throwing her entire body into gentle but well-defined motion, displayed all the riches of her contour. The sleeves of her calico gown were rolled up above the elbows, leaving her plump, muscular arms bare, and her skirt was pinned away from her really small feet and shapely ankles in such a way as to give one an idea, a suggestion, of supreme innocence and grace. Her long, crinkled gold hair was unbound, hanging far below her waist, and shining like silk. Her lips, carmine red, seemed to overflow with tender utterances.

Ever since that day I have thought churning a kind of sacred, charmingly blessed work, which ought to be, if really it is not, the pastime of those delightful beings the ancients called deities. Cream is more fragrant, more delicious, more potent than nectar or ambrosia.

A cedar churn is more delicately perfumed than any patera of the gods. And, I say it with reverence, I have seen, swaying lily-like above the churn, a beauty more perfect than that which bloomed full grown from the bright focus of the sea's ecstatic travail.

What a talk Susie and I had that day! Slowly, stealthily I crept nearer and nearer to the subject burning in my heart. I watched Susie closely, for her face was an enigma to me. I never think of her and of that day without recalling Baudelaire's dream of a giantess. More happy than the poet, I really saw my colossal beauty stand full grown before me, but, like him, I wondered—

> * * * "Si son cœur couve une sombre flamme
> Aux humides brouillards qui nagent dans ses yeux."

I could not tell, from any outward sign, what was going on in her heart. No sphinx could have been more utterly calm and mysterious. She had a most baffling way about her, too. When at last I had reached the point of a confession of my maddening love, she broke into one of my charmingest sentences to say—

"Mr. ——, you'd better move farther away from the churn or I might spatter your clothes."

This, somehow, disconcerted and bothered

me. But Susie was so calm and sweet about it, her gray eyes beamed so mysteriously innocent of any impropriety, that I soon regained my lost eloquence.

How sharply and indelibly cut in my memory, like intaglios in ivory, the surroundings of that scene, even to the minutest detail! For instance, I can see as plainly as then my new silk hat on the floor between my knees, containing a red handkerchief and a paper of chewing tobacco. I recall, also, that a sliptrod shoe lay careened to one side near the centre of the room. The bull-dog came to the door and peeped solemnly in a time or two. A string of dried pumpkin cuts hung by the fireplace, and under a small wooden table in one corner were piled a few balls of "carpet rags." I sat in a very low chair. A picture of George Washington hung above a small square window. The floor was ash boards uncarpeted. I heard some chickens clucking and cackling under the house.

Finally, I recollect it as if it were but yesterday, I said:

"I love you, Susie—I love you, and I have loved you ever since I first saw you!"

How tame the words sound now! but then they came forth in a tremulous murmur that gave them character and power. Susie looked straight at me a moment, and I thought I saw a softer light gather in her eyes. Then she took away the churn dasher and lid and fetched a large bowl from a cupboard. What a fine golden pile of butter she fished up into the bowl!

I drew my chair somewhat nearer, and watched her pat and roll and squeeze the plastic mass with the cherry ladle. A little gray kitten came and rubbed and purred round her. Again the bull-dog peeped in. A breeze gathered some force and began to ripple pleasantly through the room. Far away in the fields I heard the quails whistling to each other. An old cow strolled up the lane by the house and round the corner of the orchard, plaintively tinkling her bell. Steadily hummed Mrs. Adair's spinning wheel. I slipped my hat and my chair a little closer to Susie, and by a mighty effort directed my burning words straight to the point. I cannot repeat all I said. I would not if I could. Such things are sacred.

"Susie, I love you, madly, blindly, dearly, truly! O, Susie! will you love me—will you be my wife?"

Again she turned on me that strange, sweet,

half smiling look. Her lips quivered. The flush on her cheeks almost died out.

"Answer me, Susie, and say you will make me happy."

She walked to the cupboard, put away the bowl of butter and the ladle, then came back and stood by the churn and me. How indescribably charming she looked! She smiled strangely and made a motion with her round strong arms. I answered the movement. I spread wide my arms and half rose to clasp her to my bosom. A whole life was centred in the emotion of that moment. Susie's arms missed me and lifted the churn. I sank back into my chair. How gracefully Susie swayed herself to her immense height, toying with the ponderous churn held far above her head. I saw a kitten fairly fly out of the room, its tail as level as a gun barrel; I saw the bull-dog's face hastily withdraw from the door; I saw the carpet balls, the pumpkin cuts and the print of Washington all through a perpendicular cataract of deliciously fragrant buttermilk! I saw my hat fill up to the brim, with my handkerchief afloat. I heaved an awful sigh and leaped to my feet. I saw old Mrs. Adair standing in the partition door, with her arms akimbo, and heard her say—

"W'y, Susan Jane Samantha Ann! What 'pon airth hev ye done?"

And the Venus replied:

"I've been givin' this 'ere little woodpecker a good dose of buttermilk!"

I seized my hat and shuffled out of the door, feeling the milk gush from the tops of my boots at each hasty step I made. I ran to the gate, went through and slammed it after me. As I did so I heard a report like the closing of a strong steel trap. It was the bull-dog's teeth shutting on a slat of the gate as he made a dive at me from behind. I smiled grimly, thinking how I'd taste served in buttermilk.

On my way home I passed Ben Crane's house. He was sitting at a window playing his banjo, and singing in a stentorian voice:

"O! Woodpecker Jim,
Yer chance is mighty slim!
Jest draw yer red head into yer hole
And there die easy, dern your soul,
O! slim Woodpecker Jim!"

I was so mad that I sweat great drops of pure buttermilk, but over in the fields the quails whistled just as clear and sweet as ever, and I heard the wind pouring through the stubble as it always does in autumn!

THE LEGEND OF POTATO CREEK.

BIG yellow butterflies were wheeling about in the drowsy summer air, and hovering above the moist little sand bars of Potato Creek. A shady dell, wrapped in the hot lull of August, sent up the spires and domes of its walnut and poplar trees, clearly defined and sheeny, while underneath the forest roof the hazel and wild rose bushes had wrung themselves into dusky mats. The late violets bloomed here and there, side by side with those waxlike yellow blossoms, called by the country folk "butter and eggs." Through this dell Potato Creek meandered fantastically, washing bare the roots of a few gnarled sycamores, and murmuring among the small bowlders that almost covered its bed. It was not a strikingly romantic or picturesque place—rather the contrary—much after the usual type of ragged little dells. "A scrubby little holler" the neighborhood folk called it.

Perched on the topmost tangle of the dry, tough roots of an old upturned tree, sat little Rose Turpin, sixteen that very August day; pretty, nay beautiful, her school life just ended, her womanhood just beginning to clothe her face and form in that mysterious mantle of tenderness—the blossom, the flower that brings the rich sweet fruit of love. From her high perch she leaned over and gazed down into the clear water of the creek and smiled at the gambols of the minnows that glanced here and there, now in shadowy swarms and anon glancing singly, like sparks of dull fire, in the limpid current. Some small cray-fishes, too, delighted her with their retrograde and sidewise movements among the variegated pebbles at the bottom of the water. A small sketch book and a case of pencils lay beside her. So busy was she with her observations, that a fretful, peevish, but decidedly masculine voice near by startled her as if from a doze. She had imagined herself so utterly alone.

"Wo-erp 'ere, now can't ye! Wo, I say! Turn yer ole head roun' this way now, blast yer ole picter! No foolin', now; wo-erp, I tell ye!

Rose was so frightened at first that she seemed about to rise in the air and fly away;

but her quick glance in the direction of the sound discovered the speaker, who, a few rods farther down the creek, stood holding the halter rein of a forlorn looking horse in one hand, and in the other a heavy woodman's axe.

"Wo-erp, now! I hate like the nation to slatherate ye; but I said I'd do it if ye did'nt get well by this August the fifteenth; an' shore 'nuff, here ye are with the fistleo gittin' wus and wus every day o' yer life. So now ye may expect ter git what I tole ye! Stan' still now, will ye, till I knock the life out'n ye!"

By this time Rose had come to understand the features of the situation. The horse was sadly diseased with that scourge of the equine race, scrofulous shoulder or fistula, commonly called, among the country folk, fistleo, and because the animal could not get well the man was on the point of killing it by knocking it on the head with the axe.

Of all dumb things a horse was Rose's favorite. She had always, since her very babyhood, loved horses.

"Wo-wo-wo-erp, here! Ha'n't ye got no sense at all? Ding it, how d'ye 'spect me to hit yer blamed ole head when ye keep it a waggin' 'round in that sort o' style? Wo-erp!"

The fellow had tied the halter rein around a sapling about two feet from the ground, and was now preparing to deal the horse a blow with the axe between its eyes. The animal seemed unaware of any danger, but kept its head going from side to side, trying to fight certain bothersome gad-flies.

"O, sir, stop; don't, don't; please, sir, don't!" cried the girl, her sweet voice breaking into silvery echo fragments in every nook of the little hollow.

The man gazed all around, and, seeing no one, let fall the axe by his side. The birds, taking advantage of the silence, lifted a twittering chorus through the dense dark tops of the trees. The slimmest breath of air languidly caressed the leaves of the rose vines. The bubbling of the brook seemed to touch a mellower key, and the yellow butterflies settled all together on a little sand bar, their bright wings shut straight and sharp above their bodies. The man seemed intently listening. "Tw'an't mammy's voice, nohow," he muttered; "but I'd like to know who 'twas, though."

He stood a moment longer, as if in doubt, then again raising his axe he continued:

"Must 'a' been a jay bird squeaked. Wo-erp 'ere now! I'm not goin' to fool wi' ye all day, so hold yer head still!"

That was a critical moment for the lean, miserable horse. It lowered its head and held it quite still. The axe was steadily poised in the air. The man's face wore a look of determination—grim, stone-like. He was, perhaps, twenty-five, tall and bony, with a countenance sallow almost to greenness, sunken pale blue eyes, sun burnt hair, thin flaxy beard, and irregular, half decayed teeth. Although his body and limbs were shrunken to the last degree of attenuation, still the big cords of his neck and wrists stood out taut, suggesting great strength. The blow would be a terrible one. The horse would die almost without a struggle.

"O, O, O! Indeed, sir, you must not! Stop that, sir, instantly! You shall not do it, sir! O, sir!"

And fluttering down from her perch, Rose flew to the spot where the tragedy was pending, and cast herself pale and trembling between the horse and its would-be executioner.

The axe fell from the man's hands.

His eyes became exactly circular.

His under jaw dropped so that his mouth was open to its fullest gaping capacity. His shoulders fell till their points almost met in front of his sunken chest. He was a picture of overwhelming surprise.

High up on the dead spire of a walnut tree a woodpecker began to beat a long, rattling tattoo. The horse very lazily and innocently winked his brown eyes, and putting forth his nose sniffed at the skirt of the girl's dress.

"I'm glad—O I'm ever so glad you'll not kill him!" murmured the little lady when she saw the axe fall to the ground.

The man stood a long moment, as if petrified or frozen into position, then somewhat recovering, he re-seized the axe, and flourishing it high in the air, cried in a voice that, cracked and shrill, rang petulantly through the woods:

"I said I'd kill 'im if that garglin' oil didn't cure 'im, 'an I'm derned ef I don't, too!"

"O, sir, if you please! The poor horse is not to blame!" exclaimed the excited girl.

"'Taint no use o' beggin'; he's no 'count but to jist eat up corn, an' hay, an' paster an' the likes; and his blasted fistleo gits wus an' wus all the time. An't I spent more'n he's wo'th a tryin' to cure 'm, an' don't everybody laugh at me 'cause I've got sich a derned ole slummux of a hoss? Jist blame my picter if I'll stand it! So now you've hearn me toot my tin horn, an' ye may as well stan' out'n the way!"

"But, sir, I'll take him off your hands, may I? Say, sir? O please let me take him!"

"An' what in thunder do you want of him? What good's he goin' to do you? 'Cause, you see, he can't work nor be rid on nor nothin'."

"O never mind, sir, just please give him to me and I'll take him and care for him. Poor horsey! Poor horsey! See, he loves me already!"

The beast had thrust its nose against the maiden's hand.

"Well, I don't know 'bout this. I'd as soon 'at you have 'im as not if I hadn't swore to kill 'im, an' I musn't lie to 'im. An' besides, I've had sich a pesky derned time wi' 'im 'at it looks kinder mean 'at I shouldn't have the satisfaction of bustin' his head for it. I'm goin' to knock 'im, an' ye jist mought as well stan' aside!"

Just then the peculiarities of the man's character were written on his face. His nose denoted pugnacity, his lips sensuality, but not of a base sort, his eyes ignorance and rough kindness, his chin firmness, his jaw tenacity of purpose, and his complexion the ague. He had sworn to kill the horse, and kill him he would. You could see that in the very wrinkles of his neck. He evidently felt that it was a duty he owed to his conscience—a duty made doubly imperative by the horse's refusal to get well by the exact time prescribed.

While he stood with his axe raised, Rose was very diligently and nervously tugging at the knot that fastened the halter rein to the tree, and ere he was aware of her intent, she had untied it and was resolutely leading the poor old animal away.

The man's eyes got longest the short way as he gazed at the retreating figure.

"Well now, that's as cool as a cowcumber and twicet as juicy! Gal, ye'r' a brick! ye'r' a knot! Ye'r' a born pacer! Take 'im 'long for all I keer! Take 'im 'long!"

He put down his axe, placed his hands against his sides and smiled, as he spoke, a big wrinkling smile that covered the whole of his sallow, skinny face and ran clear down to the neck band of his homespun shirt.

"Pluck, no eend to it!" he muttered; "wonder who she is? Poorty—geeroody!"

The wild birds sang a triumphant hymn, the breeze freshened till the whole woods rustled, and louder still rose the bubbling of the stream among its bowlders.

"Well, I'll jist be dorged! The poortiest gal in all Injianny! An' she's tuck my ole hoss whether or no! She's a knot! Sort o' a cool proceedin', it 'pears to me, but she's orful welcome to the hoss! Howdsomever it's mighty much of a joke on me, 'r my name's not Zach Jones!"

He laughed long and loud. The birds laughed, too, and still the wind freshened.

The girl and the horse had quickly disappeared behind the hazel and papaw bushes. Zach Jones was alone with his axe and his reflections.

"Yender's where she sot—right up yender on that ole clay root. She must 'a' been a fishin', I reckon."

Another admiring chuckle.

He went to the spot and clambered up among the roots. There lay Rose's sketch book and pencil case. He took up the book and curiously turned the leaves, his eyes running with something like childish delight over the flowers and bits of landscape. He had never before seen a drawing.

"Poorty as the gal 'erself, 'most," he said, "an' seein' 'at she's tuck my ole hoss, I spose I'll have to take these 'ere jimcracks o' her'n. I'll take 'em 'long anyhow, jist to 'member her by!"

This argument seemed logical and conclusive, and with a quick glance over his shoulder he crammed book and pencil case into the capacious depths of the side pocket of his pants.

"Now then it's about time for my chill, an' I'd better go home. Hang the luck; s'pose I'll allus have the ager!" This last sentence was uttered in a tone of comical half despair, and accompanied by a facial contortion possible to no one but a person thoroughly saturated with ague in its chronic form.

After he left the dell, Zach had a hot walk across a clover field before he reached the dilapidated log house where he lived with his widowed mother. In a short time his chill set in, and it was a fearful one. His teeth chattered and his bony frame rattled like a bundle of dry sticks in a strong wind. After it had shaken him thus for about an hour, his brother Sammy, a lad of ten years, came in with a jug of buttermilk brought from a neighbor's.

"Mammy, 'ere's yer buttermilk," said he, setting the jug on the floor. "Shakin' like forty—a'n't ye, Zach?" he added, glancing with a sad, lugubrious smile at his brother; then, changing his tone and also his countenance, he continued, with a broader grin: "Bet ye a dollar ye can't guess what I seed over to 'Squire Martin's!"

"No, nor I don't care a cuss; so put off an' don't come yawpin' round me!" replied Zach.

"Yes ye do, too; an' I know ye do, for 'twas

yer ole fistleo hoss. That 'ere fine gal 'at stays over there is havin' a man wash 'im an' doctor 'im." Sammy winked and hitched up his pants as he spoke.

"Do say, Sammy, is that so, now?" cried the widow, holding up her hands. "How on 'arth come she by the hoss? Zach, I thought you'd killed that creater'!"

"Mammy, ef you an' Sammy 'll jist let me 'joy this 'ere ager in peace I'll be orful 'bleeged to ye," said Zach, making his chair creak and quiver with the ecstasy of his convulsion.

But Sammy's tongue would go. He thought he had a "good 'un" on Zach, and nothing short of lightning could have killed him quick enough to prevent his telling it.

"The gal says as how Zach gin 'er the ole hoss for to 'member 'im by!" he blurted out, shying briskly from Zach's foot, which otherwise would have landed him in the door yard.

"Lookee here now, Zach, you jist try the likes o' that ag'in an' I'll give ye sich a broomstickin' as ye a'n't had lately. Ye mought 'a' injured the child's insides!" and as she spoke the widow flourished the broom.

So Zach dropped his head upon his chest and employed himself exclusively with his chill. When his mother was not looking at him, however, he would occasionally slip the sketch book partly out of his pocket and peep between its leaves. When his fever came on he got "flighty" and horrified the widow with talk about an angel on a clay root and a sweet little "hoss thief" from whom he had stolen the "picters!"

I cannot exactly say how Zach got to going over to 'Squire Martin's so often after this. But his first visit was a compulsory one. His mother happening to discover his possession of the sketch book and pencil case, made him return them with his own hand to Rose. He at once became deeply interested in the progress of his former patient's convalescence; for, strange to say, the poor horse began almost immediately to get well, and in two months was sound, glossy and fat. Nor was he an ill-looking animal. On the contrary, when Rose sat on his back and stroked his mane, he arched his neck and pawed the ground like a thoroughbred.

'Squire Martin was a good man, and seeing how Zach seemed to enjoy Rose's company, he one day took the girl aside and said to her:

"You must be somewhat of a doctor, my dear, seeing how you've touched up the old hoss, and I propose for you to try your hand on another subject. There's poor Zach Jones, who's had the chills for six or eight years as constant as sunrise and sunset, and no medicine can't do him any good. Now I'll be bound if you'll try you can cure him sound and well. All you need to do in the world is to pet him up some'at as you have the ole hoss. Jist take a little interest in the feller an' he'll come out all right. All he wants is to forget he ever had the ager and take some light exercise and have some fun. Fun is the only medicine to cure the chills with. Quinine is no 'count but to make a racket in a feller's head, and calomel 'll kill 'im, sure. Now I propose to let Zach have a hoss and saddle and you must go out a riding with 'im and try to divert his mind from his sorrows and aches and pains—now that's a good girl, Rosie."

Rose, whose healthful, impulsive, generous nature would not allow her to refuse so well intended and withal so small a request, readily agreed to do all she could in the matter, and very soon thereafter she and Zach were the very best of friends, taking long rides together through woodlands and up and down the pleasant lanes of 'Squire Martin's broad estates. The young girl soon found the companionship of Zach, novel and most awkward as it was at first, agreeable and almost charming in its freshness and sincerity. As for Zach himself, he was the girl's slave from the start. He could not do too much for her in his earnest, respectful way. Women are always tyrants, and their tyranny seems to be inversely as their size and directly as the size of the man upon whom it is exerted. Rose was a very little chit of a maiden, and Zach was a great big bony frame of a fellow. The result, of course, was despotism. But, although Zach was a democrat, he seemed to like the oppression, and ran after big-winged butterflies, opened gates, pulled down and put up innumerable fences, climbed trees after empty bird nests, gathered flowers and ferns—did everything, in fact, required of him by his little queen. He became a daily visitor at the 'Squire's, and seemed to have entirely forgotten everything else or utterly submerged it in his unselfish devotion to the girl. The good 'Squire saw this with unbounded delight.

So August quietly drifted by, and September hung its yellow banner on the corn and said farewell with a sigh that had in it a smack of winter.

Rose's parents were wealthy and lived in Indianapolis, and now came the time for the girl's return to her city home. Meanwhile a remarkable change had taken place in the health and spirits of Zach Jones. The ague had departed, the sallowness was gone from his skin, somewhat of flesh had gathered on his cheeks, and in his eyes shone a cheerful light. He was straight and almost plump, and his hair and beard had assumed a gloss and liveliness they had never before known. He had thrown away quinine and calomel, and his sleep at night was soft and sweet, broken only by fair, happy dreams, that lingered long after he was awake. At home his mother had far less trouble with him, and Sammy never got a kick even if he did occasionally mention old fistleo in an equivocal way. The amount of provender it required to satisfy Zach's appetite now was a constant source of amazement to the widow.

The evening preceding Rose's departure was a fine one. The woods were gold, the sky was turquoise. Instead of riding, as usual, the young people took a stroll in the 'Squire's immense orchard. The apples were ripe and ready to be gathered into the cellars; their mellow fragrance flavored the autumn air so delicately that Zach said it smelt sweeter than an oven full of sugar cakes.

When the young folk returned from their walk the 'Squire was standing on the door step of his house. His quick eyes caught a glimpse of something unsatisfactory in the faces of the approaching couple—Zach, particularly, despite his evident effort to choke down something, discovered unmistakable signs of suffering. Rose was simply sober and thoughtful.

"What now, Zach?" asked the 'Squire, "sick, eh?" "D'know; guess I'm in for a shake; wish to the Lord it 'd shake my back bone clean out'n me!" was the reply, in a queer gurgling voice. A bunch of fall roses fell from his vest button-hole, but he did not pick it up. A hot flush, in the midst of a ghastly pallor, burned on the cheeks of the speaker. Rose tapped the ground with the toe of her kid boot, but did not speak.

The man and the girl stood there close together awhile, and the 'Squire did not catch what they said as they shook hands and parted. When Zach had gone home the 'Squire told Rose that he wished she would stay a little longer, till the ague season was over, just on Zach's account. Rose quietly replied, "I have already stayed too long;" but her voice had an infinity of pity and sorrow in it that the 'Squire did not detect.

Next morning Rose went home to the city and soon after made a brilliant *debut* in society, for she was really a charming little thing. That winter was a festive one—a season of great social activity—and some of its most direct and prominent results were a few notable marriages in the spring, among which was that of Rose to a banker of P——, Kentucky, the happy union being consummated in May.

On the very day of her wedding Rose received from her uncle the following note:

"DEAR NIECE:

"Come to see us, even if you won't stay but one day. Come right off, if you're a Christian girl. Zach Jones is dying of consumption and is begging to see you night and day. He says he's got something on his mind he wants to say to you, and when he says it he can die happy. The poor fellow is monstrous bad off, and I think you ought to be sure and come. We're all well. Your loving uncle,

"JARED MARTIN."

Something in this homely letter so deeply affected Rose that she prevailed on her husband, a few days after their marriage, to take her to 'Squire Martin's.

It was nearly sundown when the young

wife, accompanied by the 'Squire, entered the room of the dying man. He lay on a low bed by an open window, through which, with hollow hungry eyes, he was gazing into the blue distance that is called the sky of May. Birds were singing in the trees all around the house, and a cool breath of violet-scented air rippled through the window. The widow Jones, worn out with watching by the sick bed, sat sleeping in her rude arm-chair; Sammy had gone after the cow—a gift from the 'Squire.

The visitors entered softly, but Zach heard them and feebly turned his head. He put out a bloodless hand and clasped the warm fingers of Rose, pulling her into a seat by his couch. A wan smile flitted across his face as he fixed his eyes, burning like sparks in the gray ash of a spent fire, on her's, dewy with rising tears.

"The same little Rose you use to wus," he said, in a low faltering voice, that had in it an unconquerable allegiance to the one dream of his manhood. His unnaturally bright eyes ran swiftly over her face and form, then closed, as if to fasten the vision within, that it might follow him to eternity.

"The same little Rose you use to wus," he repeated, "only now you're picked off the vine an' nobody can't touch ye but the owner. I'm a poor, no 'count dyin' man, Rose, but you'll never——." His voice choked a little and he did not finish the sentence. Perhaps he thought it were better not finished.

A few moments of utter silence followed, during which, faintly, far out in the field behind the house, was heard the childish voice of Sammy, singing an old hymn, two lines of which were most distinctly heard by those in the house.

"Ah, yes—

> "This world's a wilderness of woe,
> This world it ain't my home,"

chimed in the trembling voice of the sick man. Then, by an effort that evidently taxed his fading powers to the last degree, he fixed his eyes firmly on those of the young woman. Here was a martyr of the divine sort, true and unchangeable in the flame of the torture.

"Rose, little Rose," he said, glancing uneasily at the 'Squire, "I've got something private like to say to you."

The young woman trembled. Memory was at work.

"'Squire, go out a minute, will ye?" continued Zach.

The sick man's request was promptly obeyed,

and Rose sat, drooping, alone beside the bed, while the widow snored away.

Zach now more nervously clasped the hand of the young woman. A spot of faint sunshine glimmered on the pillow close by the man's head. The out-door sounds of the wind in the young grass, and the rustle of the new soft leaves of the trees, crept into the room gently, as if not to drown the low voice of the dying man.

"It's been on my mind ever since we parted, Rose, and I ort 'a' said it then, but I choked an' couldn't; but I kin say it now and I will." He paused a moment and Rose looked pitifully at him. His chin was thrust out firmly and his lips had a determined set. He looked just as he did when about to knock the poor old horse on the head over in the dell that day. How vividly the tragic situation was recalled in Rose's mind!

"Yes, I will say it now, so I will," he resumed. "Since things turned out jist as they have, Rose, I do wish I'd 'a' paid no 'tention to ye an' jist gone on and knocked that derned ole fistleoed hoss so dead 'at he'd 'a' never kicked —I do—I do, 'i hokey! I don't want to make ye feel bad, but I'm goin' away now, an' it 'pears to me like as if I'd go easy if I know'd you'd——." He turned away his face and drew just one little fluttering breath. When, after only a few minutes' absence, the 'Squire came in, the widow still slept, the sweet air still rippled through the room, but Rose held a dead hand; Zach was at rest! The 'Squire placed his hand on the bright hair of Rose and gazed mournfully down into the pinched, pallid face of the dead. How awfully calm a dead face is!

The widow stirred in her chair, groaned, and awoke. For a moment she bent her eyes wonderingly, inquiringly on the young woman; then, rising, she clasped her in her great bony arms.

"You are the Rose, the little Rose he's been goin' on so about. O, honey, I'm orful glad you've come. You ort jist to 'a' heerd him talk about ye when he got flighty like—— but O—O—my! O Lor'! Zach—Zachy, dear! O, Miss, O, he's dead—he's dead!"

"Dead, yes, dead!" echoed the 'Squire, his words dropping with the weight of lead.

Across the fields of young green wheat ran waves of the spring wind, murmuring and sighing, while the dust of blossoms wheeled, and rose and fell in the last soft rays of the going sun. A big yellow butterfly flitted through the room.

Presently Sammy entered. He came in like a gust of wind, making things rattle with his impetuous motion.

"O, mammy! O, Zach! I's got s'thin' to tell ye, an' I'll bet a biscuit you can't guess what 't is!" he cried breathlessly.

"O, Sammy, honey, O, dear!" groaned the widow.

"S-s-h!" said the 'Squire solemnly.

"Well, I jist wanted 'm to guess," replied Sammy, "for it's awful doggone cur'u's 'at——"

"S-s-h!"

"The fistleo is broke out on Zach's ole hoss ten times as wuss as ever!"

"S-s-s-s-h!"

"It's so, for I seed it. It's layin' down over in the hollow by 'tater creek, where the ole clay root is, an' its jist about to d——."

"S-s-h!"

The child caught a glimpse of the face and was struck mute. And darkness stole athwart the earth, but the morrow's sun drove it away. Never, however, did any sun or any season chase from the heart of little Rose the shadow that was the memory of the man who died in that cabin.

STEALING A CONDUCTOR.

HE shambled into the bar-room of the hotel at Thorntown, a Boone County village, and, with a bow and a hearty "how-de do to you all," took the only vacant chair. He scratched a match and lighted his pipe. "Now we'll be bored with some sort of a long-winded story," whispered some to others of the loungers present. "Never knowed him to fail," said a lank fellow, almost loud enough for the subject to hear. "He's our travelled man," added a youth, who winked as if he were extremely intelligent and didn't mind letting folks know it.

The man himself whiffed away carelessly at his pipe, now and then raising one eye higher than the other, to take a sort of side survey of the persons present. That eye was not long in settling upon me, and after a short, searching look, gleamed in a well pleased way. He was a stout formed man of about fifty years, dressed rather seedily, and wearing a plug hat of enormous height, the crown of which was battered into the last degree of grotesqueness. He got right up, and, dragging his chair behind him, came over and settled close down in front of me.

"Stranger here, a'n't you?"

"Yes, sir."

"Your name's Fuller, a'n't it?"

"No, sir."

"Well, mebbe I'm mistaken, but you're just the picter o' Fuller. Never was a conductor on a railroad, was you?"

"Never, sir."

"Never was down in the swamps o' South-Eastern Georgy, was you?"

"Never, sir."

"Well, that beats four aces! I could 'a' bet on your bein' Fuller." He paused a moment, and then added in a very insinuating tone: "If you *are* Fuller you needn't be afeard to say so, for I don't hold any grudge 'gin you about that little matter. Now, sure enough, a'n't your name Fuller, in fact?"

I glared at the man a moment, hesitating about whether or not I should plant my fist in his eye. But something of almost child-like simplicity and sincerity beaming from his face restrained me. Surely the fellow did not wish to be as impudent as his words would imply.

"Well, stranger, I see I've got to explain, but the story's not overly long," said he, hitching up a little closer to me and settling himself comfortably.

I was about to get up and walk out of the room, when some one of the by-sitters filliped a little roll of paper to me. Unrolling it I read—

"Let him go on, he'll give you a lively one. He's a brick."

So, concluding that possibly I might be entertained, I lounged back in my seat.

"You see," said he, "I thought you was Fuller, an' Fuller was the only conductor I ever stole."

"Stole a conductor," whispered somebody, "that's a new one!"

"I've stole a good many things in my time, but I'm here to bet that no other living Hoosier ever stole a railroad conductor, an' Fuller was the only one I ever stole. I stole him slicker 'n a eel. I had him 'fore he knowed it, and you jist better bet he was one clean beat conductor fore I was done wi' 'im.

"I kin tell you the whole affair in a few minutes, and I da' say you'll laugh a good deal 'fore I'm through. You see I went down to Floridy for my health, and when I had about recivered I got onto a bum in Jacksonville and spent all my money and everything else but my very oldest suit o' clothes and my pistol, a Colt's repeater, ten inch barrel. None o' you can't tell how a feller feels in a predicament o' that sort. Somethin' got into my throat 'bout as big as a egg, and I felt kinder moist about the eyes when I had to stare the fact in the face that I was nigh onto, or possibly quite a thousand miles from home without ary a dime in my pocket. But if there's one thing I do have more 'n another in my nater it's common sense grit. Well, what you s'pose I done? W'y I jest lit out for home afoot. Well, sir, the derndest swamps is them Floridy and Georgy swamps. It's ra'lly all one swamp —the Okeefenokee. I follered the railroad that goes up to Savanny, and it led me deeper and deeper into the outlying fringes of that terrible old bog. When I had travelled a considerable distance into Georgy, and had pretty well wore my feet off up to my ankle j'ints, and was about as close onto starvation as a 'tater failure in Ireland, and when my under lip had got to hanging down like the skirt o' a wore out saddle, and when every step seemed like it'd be my last, I jest got clean despairing like and concluded to pray a little. So I got down upon my knee j'ints and put up a most extraornary supplication. I felt every word o' it, too, in all the marrer of my bones. The place where I was a prayin' was a sort o' hummock spot in a mighty bad part o' the swamp. Some awful tall pines towered stupenjisly above me. Well, jest as I was finished, and was a saying amen, the lordy mercy what a yowl something did give right over me in a tree! I think I jumped as high as your head, stranger, and come down flat-footed onto a railroad cross tie. Whillikins, how I was scared! It was one o' them whooping owls they have down there. It was while I was a running from that 'ere owl a thinkin' it was a panther, that the thought struck me somewhere in the back o' the head that I might steal a ride to Savanny on the first train 'at might pass. 'I'll try it!' says I, and so I sot right down there in the swamp and calmly waited for a train. In about a hour here come one, like the de'il a braking hemp, jist more'n a roaring through the swamp. I forgot to tell you 'at it was after dark, but the moon was dimly a shining through the fog that covers everything there o' nights. Well, here come the train, and as she passed I made a lunge at the hind platform of the last car and some how or another got onto it and away I went. It was mighty much softer 'n walking, I tell you, and I was pleased as a monkey with a red cap on. My, how fast that train did go! I could hardly hold onto where I wus. You may jist bet I clung on though, and finally I got myself setting down on the steps and then I was all hunkey. But I didn't have much time to enjoy myself there, though, for all of a sudden the light of a lantern shined on me and then somebody touched me and said—

"Ticket!"

"Mebbe you don't know how onery a feller 'll feel sometimes when he hears that 'ere word ticket—'specially when he a'n't got no ticket nor no money to pay his fare, and too, when he does want to ride a little of the derndest! That was my fix! I'd 'a' give a thousand dollars for a half dollar!

"Ticket!"

"He shook me a little this time and held his lantern down low, so's to see into my face. I know I must 'a' looked like the de'il.

"Ticket here, quick!"

"I've done paid," said I.

"Show your check then."

"Lost it," says I.

"Money, then, quick!"

"Got none," says I.

"What the —— did you git onto my train for without ticket or money? How do you expect to travel without paying, you —— lousy vagabond! You can't steal from me; out with your —— wallet and gi' me the money! Hurry up!"

"A'n't got no wallet nor no money," says I.

"Well, I'll dump you off right here, then," said he, reaching for the bell-rope to stop the train.

"For the Lord's sake let me ride to Savanny!" says I.

"A dam Northerner, I know from your voice!" said he, pulling the rope. The train began to slack and soon stopped.

"Get off!" said the conductor.

"Please l'me ride!" says I.

"Off with you!"

"Jist a few miles here on the steps!"

"Off, quick!"

"Please——"

"Here you go!" and as he said the words he tried to kick me off.

"In a second I was like a Bengal tiger. I jumped up and gethered him and we went at it. I'm as good as ever fluttered, and pretty soon I give him one flat on the nose, and we both went off 'n the platform together. As I started off I happened to think of it, so I grabbed up and pulled the bell-rope to signal the engineer to drive on. "Hoot-toot!" says the whistle, and away lick-to-split went the train, and slashy-to-splashy, rattle-o-bangle, kewoppyty-whop, bump, thud! down me and that 'ere conductor come onto a pile o' wore out cross ties in the side ditch, and there we laid a fightin'!

"But you jest bet it didn't take me long to settle *him*. He soon began to sing out ''nuff! 'nuff! take 'm off!' and so I took him by the hair and dragged him off 'n the cross ties, shot him one or two more under the ear with my fist, and then dropped him. He crawled up and stood looking at me as if I was the awfulest thing in the world. I s'pect I did look scary, for I was terrible mad. His face was bruised up mightily, but he wasn't a bleeding much. He was mostly swelled.

"Where's my train?" says he, in a sort o' blank, hollow way.

"Don't ye hear it?" I answered him, "it's gone on to Savanny!"

"Gone! who told 'm to go on? what 'd they go leave me for?"

"I pulled the bell rope," says I.

"*You?*"

"Yes, *me!*"

"What in the world did you do *that* for, man?"

"'Cause you wouldn't let me ride to Savanny!"

"What 'll I do! what 'll I do!" he cried, beginning to waltz 'round like one possessed.

"I laughed—I couldn't help it—and at the same time I pulled out my old pistol.

"Yah-hoo-a!" yelled another owl.

"For the sake o' humanity don't kill me!" said the conductor.

"I'm jest a going to shoot you a little bit for the fun o' the thing," says I.

"Mercy, man!" he prayed.

"Ticket!" says I.

"He groaned the awfulest kind, and, by the moonlight, I saw 'at the big tears was running down his face. I felt sorry for him, but I kinder thought 'at after what he'd done he'd better pray a little, so I mentioned it to him."

"I guess it mought be best if you'd pray a little," says I, cocking the pistol. My voice had a decided sepulchreal sound. The pistol clicked very sharp.

"O, kind sir," says he, "O, dear sir, I never did pray, I don't know how to pray!"

"Ticket or check!" says I, and he knowed I was talking kind o' sarcasm. "Pray quick!"

"He got down and prayed like a Methodist preacher at his very best licks. He must 'a' prayed afore.

"About the time his prayer was ended I heard a train coming in the distance. He jumped up and listened.

"Glory! Heaven be praised!" says he, capering around like a mad monkey, "they've missed me and are backing down to hunt me! where's my lantern? Have you a match? Gi'me your handkerchief!"

"Not so fast," says I; "you jest be moderate now, will you? I've no notion o' you getting on that train any more. You jest walk along wi' me, will you?"

"Where?" says he.

"Into the swamp," says I; "step off lively, too, d'you hear me?"

"O mercy, mercy, man!" says he.

"Ticket!" says I, and then he walked along wi' me into the swamp some two or three hundred yards from the railroad.

"I took him into a very thickety place, and made him back up agin a tree and put back his arms around it. Then I took one o' his suspenders and tied him hard and fast. Then I gagged him with my handkerchief. So far, so good.

"Here come the train slowly backing down, the brakesman a swinging lanterns, and the passengers all swarming onto the platforms. Poorty soon they stopped right opposite us. The conductor began to struggle. I poked the pistol in his face and jammed the gag furder into his mouth. He saw I meant work and got quiet.

"The passengers was swarming off 'n the train and I saw 'at I must git about poorty fast if I was to do anything. I soon hit on a plan. I jist stepped back a piece out o' sight o' the conductor and turned my coat, which was one o' these two-sided affairs, one side white, t'other brown. I turned the white side out. Then I flung away my greasy skull cap and took a soft hat out 'n my pocket and put it on. Then I watched my chance and mixed in with the passengers who was a hunting for the conductor.

"Strange what's become o' him," says I to a fat man, who was puffing along.

"Dim strange, dim strange," says the big fellow, in a keen, wheezing voice.

"Well, you never saw jist sich hunting as was done for that conductor. Everybody slopped around in the swamp till their clothes was as wet and muddy as mine. I was monstrous active in the search. I hunted everywhere 'cepting where the conductor was. Finally he got the gag spit out and lordy how he did squeal for help. Everybody rushed to him and soon had him free.

"It tickled me awful to hear that conductor explaining the matter. He told it something like this:

"Devil of a great big ruffian on hind platform. Asked him for ticket. Refused. Tried to put him off. Grabbed me. Smashed my nose. Flung me off. Pulled the bell-rope, then lit out on me. Mauled —— out o' me. Had a pistol two feet long. Made me pray. Heard train a coming. Took me to swamp. Tied me and sloped. Lord but I'm glad to see you all!"

"We all went aboard o' the train and I rode to Savanny onmolested. The conductor didn't mistrust me. He asked me for my check and I told him 'at I'd lost it a thrashing round in the bushes a hunting him. That was all right.

"When we got to Savanny I couldn't help letting the conductor know me, so as I passed down the steps of the car I whispered savagely in his ear:

"Ticket! dod blast you!"

"He tried to grab me as I shambled off into

the crowd, but I knowed the ropes. I heard him a shoutin'—

"There he goes! Ketch him, dern him, ketch him!" But they didn't.

"That conductor's name was Fuller, and I swear, stranger, 'at you look jest like him! Gi' me a match, will you, my pipe's out. Thanky. Hope I ha'n't bored you. Good bye all."

He shambled out and I never saw him again.

HOIDEN.

THE house was known as Rackenshack throughout the neighborhood for miles around. It was a frame structure, originally of sorry workmanship, at least thirty years old, and upon which not a cent's worth of repairing had been done since first erected, wherefore the name was peculiarly appropriate. It was not only old, rickety, paintless, half rotten and sadly sunken at one end, but the fencing around the place was broken, grown over with weeds, and slanted in as many ways as there were panels. The lawn or yard in front of the house had some old cherry trees, gnarled and decaying, growing in what had once been straight rows, but storms and more insidious vicissitudes had twisted and curled them about till they looked as though they had been thrown end foremost at the ground hap-hazard. Under and all round these trees young sprouts, from the scattered cherry seeds of many years of fruiting, had grown so thick that one could with difficulty get through them. A narrow, well-beaten path led from the gate, which lazily lolled on one hinge, up to the decayed and sunken porch, in front of which was the well, with its lop-eared windlass and dilapidated curb and shed.

A country thoroughfare, one of the old State roads leading westward to a ferry on the Wabash river near the village of Attica and eastward to either Crawfordsville, Indianapolis or Lafayette. This road was in the direct line of emigration, and in the proper seasons long lines of covered wagons rolled past, the drivers, a jolly set, hallooing to each other and bandying sharp wit and rude sarcasm at the expense of Rackenshack. Poor old house, it leered at the passers, with its windows askew, and clattered its loose boards and battered shutters in utter and complacent defiance of all their jeers!

Rackenshack belonged to Luke Plunkett and Betsy, his sister; the latter an old maid beyond all cavil, the former a bachelor of about thirty. The lands of the estate were pretty broad, comprising some two thousand acres of rich prairie and "river bottom" land, which had been kept in a much better state of improvement than the house had. In fact, Luke was considered a careful, industrious, frugal farmer. He had large, well regulated barns and stock sheds and stables—plenty of fine horses, cattle, hogs, sheep and mules, all well fed and cared for, and it was generally understood that he had a pretty round deposit in a bank.

Perhaps 'Squire Rube Fink, sometimes called "the Rev. Major Fink" and sometimes "Talking Rube," gives the best description of Luke's condition, habits and surroundings, that I can offer. It is truthful and singularly graphic. He says:

"Luke Plunkett's no fool if he does live at Rack-a-me-shack and 'spect the ole rotten tabernacle to fall down on him every time a rooster crows close by. That feller's long-headed, he is. To be sure, sartinly, his barn's a dern sight better 'n his house, but his head's level, for, d'ye see, that's the way to make money. A house don't never make no money for a feller—it's nothin' but dead capital to put money into a fine dwellin'. Luke's pilin' his money in the bank. He's been doin' a sharp thing in wheat and live stock at Cincinnati, and I guess he knows what he's about. He don't keer about what sort o' house he lives in. But I tell you that red haired sister o' his'n is lightning. She's what bosses the job all round that ole shanty; but she can't red-hair it over Luke in the farm matters. He has his own way. He's so quiet and peculiar; a still, say nothin', bull-dog sort o' man he is."

Indeed, Luke was one of that quiet sort of men who, without ever once loudly asserting a right or disputing any word you say, invariably go ahead on their own judgment and carry their point in everything. Nevertheless, he was a man of fine, generous nature at bottom, a good brother and a worthy friend.

But it was with Luke just as it is, more or less, with us all. He absorbed into his life the spirit of his surroundings. He grew somewhat to resemble Rackenshack in outward appearance. He became slovenly in his dress and let his hair and beard grow wild. His naturally handsome face gradually took on a sort of good humored ugliness, and his heavy shoulders slanted over like the uneven gables of his house He became an inveterate chewer and smoker of tobacco. What time a quid of the weed was not in his mouth, the short thick stem of a dark, nicotine-coated briar-root pipe took its place there.

Luke was an early riser; therefore it happens that our story properly begins on a fine June morning, just before sunrise. The birds seemed to suspect that a story was to date from that hour, for they were up earlier than usual and made a great rustle of wings and a sweet Babel of voices in the old cherry trees. There were the oriole, the cat bird, the yellow throat, the brown thrush and the red bird, all putting forth at once their charmingest efforts. The old cherry trees, knee deep in the foliage of their under growing seedlings, gleamed dusky green in the early light, as Luke, bare-headed, barefooted and in his "shirt sleeves," as the phrase goes, issued from the front door of Rackenshack, and walked down the path across the yard to the gate at the road. Of late he had been in the habit of "taking a smoke" the first thing after getting up in the morning, and somehow the gate, though off one hinge and having doubtful tenure of the other, was his favorite thing to lean upon while watching the whiffs of blue smoke slowly float away.

On this particular morning he seemed a little agitated; and, indeed, he was vexed more deeply than he had ever before been. Just the preceding evening he had learned that a corps of civil engineers were rapidly approaching his premises with a line of survey, and that the purpose was to locate and build a railway right through the middle of his farm.

To Luke the very idea was outrageous. He felt that he could never stand such an imposition. His land was his own, and when he wanted it dug up and leveled down and a track laid across it he would do it himself. He did not want his farm cut in two, his fields disarranged and his fences moved, nor did he wish to see his live stock killed by locomotives. The truth is he was bitterly opposed to railroads, any how. They were innovations. They were enemies to liberty. They brought fashion, and spendthrift ways, and speculation, and all that along with them. Other folks might have railroads if they wanted them, but they must not bother him with them. He could take care of his affairs without any railroads. Besides, if he wanted one he could build it. He hung heavily upon the gate, thinking the matter over, and would not have bestowed a second glance at the carriage that came trundling past if he had not caught the starry flash of a pair of blue eyes and a rosy, roguish girl's face within. The beauty of that countenance struck the great rough fellow like a blow. He stared in a dazed, bewildered way. He took his pipe from his mouth and involuntarily tried to hide his great big bare feet behind the gate post. He felt a queer, dreamy thrill steal all over him. It was his first definite impression of feminine beauty. Instantly that round, happy, mischievous face, with its dimples and indescribable shining lines of half latent mirth, set itself in his heart forever.

The carriage trundled on in the direction of the ferry. Luke followed it with his eyes till it disappeared round a turn in the road; then he put the pipe to his mouth again and began puffing vigorously, wagging his head in a way that indicated great confusion of mind. There are times when a glimpse of a face, the sudden half-mastering of a new, grand idea, a view of a rare landscape or even a cadence in some new tune, will start afresh the long dried up wells of a heart. Something like this had happened to Luke.

"Sich a gal! sich a gal!" he murmured from the corner of his mouth opposite his pipe stem. "I don't guess I'm a dreamin' now, though I feel a right smart like it. I *hev* dreamed of that 'ere face though, many of times. I've seed it in my sleep a thousand times, but I never s'posed 'at I'd see it shore enough when I'd be awake! Sweetest dreams I ever had—sweetest face God ever made! I wonder who she is?" As if to supplement Luke's soliloquy at this point, a cardinal red bird flung out from the dusky depths of the oldest cherry tree an ecstatic carol, and a swallow, swooping down from the clear purple heights, almost touched the man's cheek with its shining wings, and the sun lifted its flaming face in the east and flooded the fields with gold.

Luke turned slowly toward the old house. The breeze that came up with the sun poured through the orchard with a broad, joyous surge, while something like blowing of strange winds and streaming of soft sunlight made strangely happy the inner world of the smitten Hoosier. His big strong heart fluttered mysteriously. He actually took his pipe from his lips and broke into a snatch of merry song, that startled Betsy, his sister, from her morning nap.

For the time the hated railroad survey was forgotten. The landscape at Rackenshack, as if by a turn of the great prisms of nature, suddenly took on rainbow hues. The fields flashed with jewels, and the woods, a wall of dusky emerald, were wrapped in a roseate mist, stirred into dreamy motion by the breeze. A light, grateful fragrance seemed to pervade all space, as if flung from the sun to soften and enhance the charm of his gift of light and heat. Such a hold did all this take upon Luke, and so utterly abstracted was he, that when breakfast was ready Betsy was obliged to remind him of the fact that he had neglected to wash his face and hands, and comb his hair and beard—things absolutely prerequisite to eating at her table.

"Forgot it, sure's the world," said Luke; "don't know what ever possessed me."

"Maybe you've forgot to turn the cows into the milk stalls, too?" said Betsy.

"If I ha'n't I'm a gourd!" and Luke scratched his head distractedly.

"What 'd I tell you, Luke Plunkett? It's come at last, O lordy! You're as crazy as a June bug all along of smoking that old pipe! Rot the nasty, stinking old thing! It's a perfect shame, Luke, for a man to just smoke what little brains he's got clean out. You ought to be ashamed of yourself, so you ought!"

While she was speaking Betsy got the big wooden washbowl for her brother, whereupon he proceeded to make his ablutions in a most energetic way, taking up great double handfuls of water and sousing his face therein with loud puffings, that enveloped his head in a cloud of spray.

When a clean tow linen towel had served its purpose, Luke remarked:

"Don't know but what I *am* some'at crazy in good earnest, Betsy, since I come to think it all over. I'm r'ally onto it a right smart. What 'd you think, Betsy, if I'd commence talkin' 'oman to ye?"

"Luke, Luke! are you crazy? Is your mind clean gone out of your poor smoky head?"

"That's not much of a answer to my question."

"Well, what *do* you mean, *anyhow?*"

"I mean business, that's what!"

"Luke!"

"Yes 'm."

"Do try to act sensible now. What is it, Luke? What makes your eyes look so strange and dance about so? What do you mean by all this queer talk?"

Luke finished combing, and, going to the table, sat down and was proceeding to discuss the fried chicken and coffee without further remark, but Betsy was not so easily balked. She, like most red haired women, wished her questions to be fully and immediately answered, wherefore some indications of a storm began to appear.

Luke smiled a quiet little smile that had hard work getting out through his beard.

Betsy trotted her foot under the table. Her hand trembled as she poured the coffee—trembled so violently that she scalded her left thumb. It was about time for Luke to speak or have trouble, so, in a very gentle voice, he said:

"Well, I saw a gal—a gal an' her father, I reckon—go by this mornin'."

"Well, what of it? S'pose there's plenty of girls and their fathers, ain't there?" snapped Betsy.

Luke drew a chicken leg through his mouth, laid down the bone, leered comically at his sister from under his bushy eyebrows, and said:

"But the gal was purty, Betsy—purty as a pictur', sweet as a peach, juicy an' temptin' as a ripe, red cored watermillion! You can't begin to guess how sweet an' nice she did look. My heart just flolloped and flopped about, an' it's at it yet!"

"Luke Plunkett, you *are* crazy! You're just as distracted as a blind dog in high rye. Drink a cup of hot coffee, Luke, and go lie down a bit, you'll feel better." The spinster was horrified beyond measure. She really thought her brother crazy.

The man finished his meal in silence, smiling

the while more grimly than before, after which he took his shot gun and a pan of salt and trudged off to a distant field to salt some cattle. He always carried his gun with him on such occasions, and not unfrequently brought back a brace of partridges or some young squirrels. As he strode along, thinking all the time of the girl in the carriage, he suddenly came upon a corps of engineers with transit, level, rod and chain, staking out, through the centre of a choice field, a line of survey for a railroad. In an instant he was like a roaring lion. He glared for a second or so at the intruders, then lowering his gun he charged them at a run, storming out as he did so:

"What you doin' here, you onery cusses, you! Leave here! Get out! Scratch! Sift! Dern yer onery skins, I'll shoot every dog of ye! Git out 'n here, I say—out, out!"

The corps stampeded at once. The surveyor seized his transit, the leveller his level, the rod man his rod, the axe men and chain men their respective implements, and away they went, "lick-to-split, like a passel o' scart hogs," as Luke afterwards said, "as fast as they could ever wiggle along!"

No wonder they ran, for Luke looked like a demon of destruction. It was a wild race for the line fence, a full half mile away. The leveler, being the hindmost man, rolled over this fence just as a heavy bowlder, hurled by Luke, struck the top rail. It was a close shave, a miss of a hair's breadth, a marvelous escape. Luke rushed up to the fence and glared over at his intended victims. Here he knew he must stop, for he doubted the legality of pursuing them beyond the confines of his own premises. Somewhat out of breath he leaned on the fence and proceeded to swear at the corps individually and collectively, shaking his fists at them excitedly, till the appearance of a new man on the scene made him start and stare as if looking at a ghost. He was a well dressed, gentlemanly appearing person of about the age of forty-five, pale and thoughtful—calm, gray eyed, commanding. Luke recognized him at once as the man he had seen in the carriage, and, indeed, the vehicle itself stood hard by, with a beautiful, laughing, roguish face looking out of one of the windows. The lion in the stalwart farmer was quelled in an instant. He felt his legs grow weak. He set his gun by the fence and touched his hat to the little lady.

"Your name, I believe, is Luke Plunkett?" said the approaching gentleman.

"Yes, sir," said Luke.

"You own two thousand acres of land here?"

"Yes, sir."

"Your residence is called Rackenshack?"

"Yes, sir." (Suppressed titter from the carriage.)

"So I thought. Pull back, men (addressing the corps), pull back to where you dropped the line and bring it right along. Mr. Plunkett will not harm you now."

The corps began to move. Luke fiercely seized his gun; but before he could lift it or utter a word, a ten-inch Colt's repeater was thrust into his face by the calm gentleman, and a steady hand held it there.

"Mr. Plunkett," said the man, "I am the chief engineer of the —— Railroad. I am making a location. The laws of this State give me the right to go upon your land with my corps and have the survey made. I am not to be trifled with. If you offer to cock that gun I'll put six holes through you. What do you say, now?"

The voice was that of a cold man of business. There was a coffin in every word. The muzzle of the pistol steadily covered Luke's left eye. The situation was rigid. Luke hesitated—his face ashy with anger and fear, his eyes alternating their glances between the muzzle of the pistol and that wonderful shining face at the carriage.

"Shoot him, papa, shoot him! Shoot him!" Sweet as a silver bell rang out the girl's voice, more like a ripple of idle song than a murderous request, and then a clear, happy laugh went echoing off through the woods in which the carriage stood.

Slowly, steadily, Luke let fall the breech of his gun upon the ground beside him. The engineer smiled grimly and lowered his pistol, while the corps, headed by the surveyor, took up its line of march to the point where work had been so suddenly left off.

The young lady clapped her tiny white hands for joy.

A big black woodpecker began to cackle in a tree hard by.

Luke felt like a man in a dream.

The whole adventure, so far, had been clothed in most unreal seeming.

It can hardly be told how, by rapid transitions from one thing to another in his talk, the engineer drew Luke's mind away from the late difficulty and gradually aroused in him a kindly feeling. In less than ten minutes the two men were sitting side by side on a log, smoking cigars from the engineer's pouch and chatting calmly, amicably.

Luke's eyes often rested steadily fixed in the direction of the carriage. Through the thin veil of tobacco smoke the face of the young girl seemed to the farmer angelic in its beauty. All around the sweets of summer rose and fell, and drifted like scarcely visible shining mists, fraught with the spice of leaf and perfume of blossom, agitated by swells of tricksy wind, going on and on to the mysterious goal of the season.

The two men talked on until the corps had pushed the line of survey far past them into the cool, shady deeps of the woods, whence their voices came back fainter and fainter every moment. At length the engineer arose, and stretching out his hand to Luke, said:

"Mr. Plunkett, I'm sure I'll be able to serve you some time; let us be friends. I shall be in this vicinity most of the time till the road is built. No doubt I can show a way to profit by the construction of a railroad across your land. If you are sharp it will make your fortune. I like your independent way, sir, and hope to know you better. Here is my card."

Luke took the bit of pasteboard without saying a word. They shook hands and the engineer got into his carriage.

"Here's my card, too, Mr. Plunkett," cried the girl. She said something more, but the horses were made to plunge rapidly away, and the words were lost; but the flash of a white jewelled hand caught Luke's eye as a delicately tinted card came fluttering towards him. He sprang and seized it. If a bag of diamonds had been flung at his feet he could not have been more excited. His hands trembled. All the incidents of the only fairy tale he had ever read came at once into his mind. He stood with his feet turned in, like some great awkward boy, a bashful, shame-faced look lurking about his mouth and eyes. He filled his pipe and lighted it from the stump of his cigar with nervous eagerness. A squirrel came down to the lowest limbs of a beech tree hard by and barked at him, but he did not notice it. He read the names on the cards:

"*Elliot Pearl, C. E.*"
"*Hoiden Pearl.*"

The first printed in small capitals, the second written in a delicate, rather cramped feminine hand. He stood for a long time dreamily employed in turning these bits of paper over and over. His thoughts were so vague in outline and so dim in filling up that they cannot be reproduced. They slipped away on the summer air, like little puffs of perfume, and were lost, to be found by many and many a one in the ineffable places of dreamland. Finally, shaking himself as if to break the charm that held him in its meshes, he took up his gun and slowly made his way homeward. All along his walk he kept smiling to himself and talking aloud, but his words were such that it would be sacrilege to repeat them now. Let them hover about in the sunlight of summer, where he uttered them, as things too delicate to be pressed between the lids of a book.

Betsy had trouble with Luke for some days after this. He lay about the house, saying little, eating little, giving little attention to the many tenants who worked his estate. He was in good health, was not in trouble (so he said to his sister), but he did not care to be bothered with business. He was tired and would rest awhile. "He smoked pretty near all the time," as Betsy declared. But not a hint fell from his lips as to what might be running in his mind.

So the days slipped past till July hung golden mists on the horizon and filled the woods with that rare stillness and dusky slumbrousness that follows the maturing of the foliage and the coming on of fruit. The cherry trees at Rackenshack had grown ragged and dull, and the birds, excepting a few swallows wheeling about the old chimney tops, had all flown away to the woods and fields. The wheat had been cut and stacked, the corn had received its last ploughing. Still Luke hung about the house annoying Betsey with his pipe and his utter carelessness. That he was "distracted" Betsy did not for a moment doubt. She used every means her small stock of wit could invent to urge him out of his singular mood, but without avail. He took to the few old novels he could find about the house, but sometimes he would gaze blankly at a single paragraph for a whole hour.

One morning as he lay on the porch, his head resting upon the back of a chair, reading, or pretending to read an odd volume of "The Scottish Chiefs," a little boy, 'Squire Brown's son, came to bring home a monkey-wrench his father had borrowed some time before. The boy was a bright, rattle-box, say-everything, pop-eyed sort of child, and was not long telling all the news of the neighborhood. Luke gave little attention to what he was saying, till at length he let fall something about a young lady—a fine, rich young lady, staying at Judge Barnett's—a young lady who could outrun him, out jump him, beat him playing marbles and ball, who could climb away up in the June apple tree, who could ride a colt bare-back, who could beat Jim Barnett shooting at a mark, who could, in fact, do a half a hundred things to perfection that strict persons would think a young lady should never do at all, but which seemed to make a heroine of her in the narrator's boyish view.

"What's the gal's name?" queried Luke in a slow, lazy way, but his eyes shot a gleam of hope.

"Hoidy Pearl," replied the lad.

Hoiden Pearl! That name had been woven into every sound that had reached Luke's ears for days and nights and nights together, and now, like a sweet tune nearly mastered, it took a deeper, tenderer meaning as the boy pronounced it in his childish way.

"Hoidy Pearl is her name," the lad continued. "She's come to stay at the Judge's all summer till the new railroad's finished. Her father's the boss of the road. She's jest the funniest girl, o-o-e! And she likes me, too!"

Luke raised himself to a sitting posture and looked at the boy so earnestly that he drew back a pace or two as if afraid.

"Boy, you're not lyin', are ye?" said the man in a low, earnest tone.

"No I'm not, neither," was the quick reply.

Luke got up, flung aside his book and strolled off into the woods. Wandering there in the cool, silent places, he dreamed his dream. For hours he sat by a little spring stream in the dense shadow of a big cotton-wood tree. The birds congregated about him, and chirped and sang; the squirrels came out chattering and frisking from branch to branch; but he gave them no look of recognition—he saw them not, heard them not. The birds might have lit upon his head and the squirrels might have run in and out of his pockets with impunity. He smoked all the time, refilling and relighting his pipe whenever it burned out. He did not know how much he was smoking, nor that he was smoking at all. A bright face set in a mass of yellow curls, a wee white hand all spangled with jewels, a voice sweeter than any bird's, a name—Hoiden Pearl—these rang, and danced, and echoed, and shone in the recesses of his brain and heart to the exclusion of all else. He was trying to think, but he could not. He wanted to mature a plan, but not even an outline could find room in his head. It was full. Strange, indeed, it may seem, that a rough farmer of Luke's age should thus fall into the ways of the imaginative, sentimental stripling; but, after all, the fit must come on some time in life. No doubt it goes harder with some constitutions than with others. Luke may have been unwittingly strongly predisposed that way. Neither the exterior of a man nor his surroundings will do to judge him by. Nature is that mysterious in all her ways. Luke talked aloud, sometimes gesticulating in a quiet way.

"I *must* see the gal—I *will* see the gal," he muttered at last. "It's no use talkin', I jist will see her!"

Suddenly a light broke from his face He smiled like one who has victory in his grasp—like an editor who has an idea, like a reviewer who has found some bad verse. He got up immediately, went back to the barn, hitched a horse to a small road wagon and drove to town. There he spent time and money with a merchant tailor and other vendors of clothing. He was very fastidious in his selection. Nothing but the finest would do him. A few days after this he brought home a trunk full of princely raiment—broad cloth and fine linen. Betsy was struck dumb with amazement when the trunk was opened. A dream of such costly things, such reckless extravagance, would have driven her mad. Silent, open-eyed, wondering, she came in and stood behind Luke while he was unpacking. He looked up presently and saw her. His face flushed violently, and in a half-whining, half-ashamed tone he muttered:

"Now, Betsy, you jest git out'n here faster'n ye come in, for I'm not goin' to stan' no foolin' at all, now. These 'ere's my clothes and paid for out'n my money, an' I'm the jedge of what I need. I ha'n't had any good duds for a long time, and I'm tired o' lookin' like a scarecrow made out'n a salt bag. I've been thinkin' for a long time I'd git these 'ere things, an' now I've got 'm. You kin git you some if ye like, but I don't want ye a standin' round here gawpin' at me on 'count o' my clothes; so you go off an' mind yer own affairs. It's no great sight to see some shirts, an' coats, and pants, an' collars, an' vests, an' sich like, is it?"

Before this speech was finished Betsy had backed out of the room and closed the door. As she did so she let go a sigh that came back to Luke like a Parthian arrow; but it happened just then that he was holding up in front of him a buff linen vest which kept the missile from his heart.

He dressed himself with great care, and an hour later he slipped out of the house unseen, and took his way towards the rather pretentious residence of Judge Barnett, the gables of which, a mile away, gleamed between rows of Lombardy poplars. The Judge was one ot those half cultivated men who, in every country neighborhood, pass for prodigies of learning and ability. He was the autocrat of the county in political and social affairs—one ot those men who really know a great deal, but who arrogate more. He got his title from having been County Commissioner when the court house was building. Some said he made money out of the transaction, but our story is silent there.

It would have been an interesting study for a philosopher to have watched Luke throughout the singular ramble he took that morning. It would have been such a manifest revelation of the state of the fellow's feelings. It would have minutely disclosed, and more eloquently than any verbal confession, the rise and fall, the ebb and flow, the alternating strength and weakness of his purpose, and the will behind it. Then, too, it would have let fall delightful hints of the unselfishness of his new and all-engrossing passion, and of the charming simplicity and sincerity of his great rugged nature at its inner core. At first he struck out boldly a direct line to Judge Barnett's residence, his face beaming with the light of settled happiness, but as he neared the pleasant grounds surrounding the house he began to discover some trepidation. His gait wavered, the expression of his face shifted with each step, and soon his course was indeterminate—a fitful sauntering from this place to that—a tricksy, uneven flight, like that of a lazy butterfly, if one may indulge the comparison—a meandering in and out among the trees of a small walnut grove—a strolling here and there, now along the verge of a well set old orchard, now down the low hedge behind the garden, and anon leaning over the board fence that inclosed the Judge's ample barn and stable lot; he gazed wistfully, half comically, in the direction of the upper windows of the farm house. It was one of those peculiarly yellow days of summer, when everything swims in a golden mist. The blue birds floated aimlessly about from stake to stake of the fences; the wind, felt only in jerky puffs, blew no particular way, and as idly and as eccentrically as any blue bird, and in full accord with the fitful will of the wind, Luke drifted through the sheen of summer all round Barnett Place. He lazed about, humming a tune, and, for a wonder, not smoking—half restless, half contented, looking for something, scarcely expecting anything. When once a great rough man does get into a childish way, he is a child of which ordinary children would be ashamed, and just then Luke, the big bashful fellow, was an instance strikingly in point. Occasionally he talked half aloud to himself. Once, while lounging on the orchard fence, gazing down between the long rows of russet and pippin trees, he said dreamily,

"I *must* see her. I can't go back 'ithout seein' her." It so chanced that just then a shower of blackbirds fell upon the orchard, covering the trees and the ground, flying over and over each other, twittering and whistling as only blackbirds can. Their wings smote together with a tender rustling sound like that of a spring wind in young foliage, or of a thousand lovers whispering together by moonlight. Luke watched them a long while, a doleful shade gathering in his face. "The little things loves each other," he muttered; "everything loves something; an' jest dern my lights ef I don't love the gal, an' I'm boun' to see her!" Seemingly nerved by sudden resolution, he climbed over the fence and started at a slashing pace across the orchard towards the house, scaring all the birds into an ecstasy of flight, so that they dashed themselves against the foliage of the apple trees, making it rustle and sway as if blown on by a strong wind. He did not keep on, however. His resolution seemed to burn out about midway the orchard. He began to drift around again, his pace becoming slower and slower. His shoulders drooped forward as if burdened with a great load, his eyes turned restlessly from side to side.

"I jest can't do it!" he murmured—"I jest can't do it, an' I mought as well go back!" There was a petulant ring to his voice—a nervous, worried tone, that had despair in it.

Out of a June apple tree right over his head fell a sweet, silvery, half child's, half woman's voice, that thrilled him through every fibre to the marrow of his bones.

"What's the matter, Goosey?" What have you lost? What are you hunting for? Want a good apple?"

Luke looked up just in time to catch squarely on his nose a fine, ripe June apple, and through a mist of juice and a sheeny curtain of leaves he saw the lovely face he had come to look for. A thump on the nose from an apple, no matter if it is ripe and soft, is a little embarrassing, and it only makes it more so when the racy wine of the fruit flies into one's eyes and all over one's new clothes. But there are moments of supreme bliss when such a mishap passes unnoticed. Luke felt as if the blow had been the touch of a magician conjuring up a scene that held him rapt and speechless.

"O, my! I didn't go to hit you! Please excuse me, sir—do. I thought you 'd catch it in your hands."

She came lightly down from the tree, descending like a bird, easily, gracefully, as if she had been born to climb. She murmured many apologies, but the genius of fun danced in her saucy, almost impertinent eyes, belying her regretful words. Luke looked down at her dazed and speechless. She, however, was full of prattle—half childish, half womanly, half serious, half bantering—her eyes upturned to his, her voice a very bird's in melody. In the more innocent sense of the word she looked like her name, Hoiden. Nothing unchaste or indelicate about her appearance; just a sort of want of restraint; a freedom that amounted to an utter lack of responsibility to the ordinary claims and dictates of propriety. A close, trained, intelligent observer would have seen at once that she was wilful, spoiled, unbridled, but not bad, not in the least vicious; really innocent and full of good impulses. She was beautiful, too—wonderfully beautiful—just on the hither side of womanhood, plump, budding, bewitching. How she did it can never be known, but she soon had Luke racing with her all over the orchard. They climbed trees together, they scrambled for the same apple, they laughed, and shouted, and played till the horn at the farmhouse called the field hands to dinner. They parted then, as children part, promising to meet again the next day. The girl's cheeks were rosy with exercise, so were Luke's.

How strange! Day after day that great, bearded, almost middle-aged, uncouth farmer went and played slave to that chit of a girl, doing whatever ridiculous or childish thing she proposed, caring for nothing, asking for nothing but to be with her, listen to her voice and feast his eyes upon her beauty. He gladly bore everything she heaped upon him, and to be called "Goosey" by her was to him inexpressibly charming.

Betsy's womanly nature was not to be deceived. She soon comprehended all; but she dared not mention the subject to Luke. He was in no mood to be opposed. So he went on—and Betsv sighed.

The summer softened into autumn. The maple leaves reddened. The long grass turned brown and lolled over. A softness and tenderness lurked in the deep blue sky, and the air had a sharp racy fragrance from ripe fruit and grain. Meantime the railroad had been pushed with amazing rapidity nearly to completion. Every day long construction trains went crashing across Luke's farm. Passenger coaches were to be put on in a few days. Luke was the very picture of happiness. He seemed to grow younger every day. His worldly prospects, too, were flattering. A station had been located on his land, around which a town had already begun to spring up. The vast value of Luke's timber, walnut and oak, was just beginning to appear; indeed, immense wealth lay in his hands. But his happiness was of a deeper and purer sort than that generated by simple pecuniary prosperity. Hoiden Pearl was in the focus of all his thoughts; her face lighted his dreams, her voice made the music that charmed him into a wonderland of bliss. He said little about her, even to Betsy, but it needed no sharpness of sight to discover from his face what was going on in his heart. He had even forgotten his pipe. He had not smoked since that first day in the orchard. He had straightened up and looked a span taller.

The girl did not seem to dream of any tender attachment on Luke's part. In fact he gave her no cause for it. He fed on his love inwardly and never thought of telling it. To be with her was enough. It satisfied all his wants. She was frank and free with him, but tyrannized over him—ordered him about like a servant, scolded him, flattered him, pouted at him, smiled on him, indeed kept him crazy with rapture all the time. Once only she became confidentially communicative. It was one day, sitting on an old mossy log in the Judge's woodland pasture, she told him the story of her past life. How thrillingly beautiful her face became as it sobered down with the history of early orphanage! Her father had died first; then her mother, who left her four years old in the care of Mr. Pearl, her paternal uncle, with whom she had ever since been, going from place to place, as the calls of his nomadic profession made it necessary, from survey to survey, from this State to that, seeing all sorts of people, and receiving her education in small, detached parcels. The story was a sad, unsatisfactory one, breathing neglect, yet full of a certain kind of sprightliness, and touched here and there with the fascination of true romance.

It is hard to say when Luke would have awakened from his tender trance to the strong reality of love. He was too contented for self-questioning, and no act or word of Hoiden's invited him to consider what he was doing or whither he was drifting.

It was well for Luke and the girl, too, that it was a sparsely settled neighborhood, for evil tongues might have made much of their constant companionship and childish behavior.

As for the Judge, after it was all over he admitted that he felt some qualms of conscience about allowing such unlimited intimacy to go on, but he excused himself by saying that the girl, when confined to the house, was such an unmitigated nuisance that he was glad for some one to monopolize her company.

"Why," said he, in his peculiar way, "she set the whole house by the ears. She made more clatter and racket than a four-horse Pennsylvania wagon coming down a rocky hill. She would go from garret to cellar like a whirlwind and twist things wrong side out as she went—— she was a tart!"

But at length, toward the middle of autumn the end came. Luke had business with some hog-buyers in Cincinnati, whither he was gone several days. Meantime the railroad was completed, and Mr. Pearl came to the Judge's early one morning and called for Hoiden. His business with his employers was ended, and he had just finished an arrangement that had long been on foot to go to one of the South American States and take charge of a vast engineering scheme there. The girl was de lighted. Such a prospect of travel and adventure was enough to set one of her temperament wild with enthusiasm. She flew to packing her trunk, her face radiant with joy.

Only an hour later Mr. Pearl and Hoiden stood at the new station on Luke's land, waiting for the east-going train. Mr. Pearl happened to think of a business message he wished to leave for Luke, so he went into the depôt building and wrote it. When Hoiden saw the letter was for Luke she begged leave to put in a few words of postscript, and she had her way.

The train came and the man and girl were whirled away to New York, and thence they took ship for South America, never to return.

Next day Luke came back, bringing with him a beautifully carved mahogany box mounted in silver. Betsy met him at the door, and, woman-like, told the story of Hoiden's departure almost at the first breath.

"Gone all the way to South America," she added, after premising that she would never return.

A peculiarly grim, grayish smile mantled the face of Luke. He swallowed a time or two before he could speak.

"Come now, sis" (he always said "sis" when he felt somewhat at Betsy's mercy), "come now, sis, don't try to fool me. I'm goin' right over to see the gal now, an' I've got what'll tickle her awfully right here in this 'ere box."

Out in the yard the blue jays and woodpeckers were quarrelling over the late apples heaped up by the cider mill. The sky was clear, but the sunlight, coming through a smoky atmosphere, was pale, like the smile of a sick man. The wind of autumn ran steadily through the shrubby weedy lawn with a sigh that had in it the very essence of sadness.

"I tell you, Luke, I'm not trying to fool you; they've gone clean to South America to stay always," reiterated Betsy.

Luke gazed for a moment steadily into his sister's eyes, as if looking for a sign. Slowly his stalwart body and muscular limbs relaxed and collapsed. The box fell to the floor with a crash, where it burst, letting roll out great hoops of gold and starry rings and pins—a gold watch and chain, a beautiful gold pen and pencil case, and trinkets and gew-gaw things almost innumerable. They must have cost the full profits of his business trip.

Luke staggered into a chair. Betsy just then happened to think of the letter that had been left for her brother. This she fetched and handed to him. It was the note of business from Mr. Pearl. There was a postscript in a different hand:

"*Good-bye, Goosey!*
Hoidy Pearl."

That was all. Luke is more morose and petulant than he used to be. He is decaying about apace with Rackenshack, and he smokes constantly. He is vastly wealthy and unmarried.

Betsy is quiet and kind. Up stairs in her chest is hidden the mahogany coffer full of golden testimonials of her brother's days of happiness and the one dark hour of his despair!

THE PEDAGOGUE.

HE was one of the farmer princes of Hoosierdom, a man of more than average education, a fluent talker and ready with a story. Knowing that I was looking up reminiscences of Hoosier life and specimens of Hoosier character, he volunteered one evening to give me the following, vouching for the truth of it. Here it is, as I "short-handed" it from his own lips. I omit quotation marks.

The study of one's past life is not unlike the study of geology. If the presence of the remains of extinct species of animals and vegetables in the ancient rocks calls up in one's mind a host of speculative thoughts touching the progress of creation, so, as we cut with the pick of retrospection through the strata of bygone days, do the remains of departed things, constantly turning up, put one into his studying cap to puzzle over specimens fully as curious and interesting in their way as the *cephalaspis*.

The first stratum of my intellectual formation contains most conspicuously the remains of dog-eared spelling books, a score or more of them by different names, among which the *Elementary* of Webster is the best preserved and most clearly defined. It was finding an old, yellow, badly thumbed and dirt soiled copy of Webster's spelling book in the bottom of an old chest of odds and ends, on the fly-leaf of which book was written "T. Blodgett," that lately brightened my memory of the things I am about to tell you.

The old time pedagogue is a thing of the past—*pars temporis acti* is the Latin of it, may be, but I'm not sure—I'm rusty in the Latin now. When I quit school I could read it a good deal. But of the pedagogue. The twenty years since he ceased to flourish seem, on reflection, like an age—an *æon*, as the Greeks would say. I never did know much Greek. I got most of my education from pedagogues of the old sort. They kept pouring it on to me till it soaked in. That's the way I got it. I have had corns and bunions on my back for not being sufficiently porous to absorb the multiplication table rapidly enough to suit the whim of one of those learned tyrants. But the pedagogue became extinct and passed into the fossil state some twenty years ago, when free schools took good hold. He scampered away when he heard the whistle of the steam engine along iron highways and the cry of small boys on the streets of the towns hawking the daily papers. He could live nowhere within the pale of innovation. He was born an exemplar of rigidity. The very name of reform was hateful to him. We older fellows remember him well, but to the younger fry he is not even a fossil, he is a myth. Of course pedagogues differed slightly in the matter of particular disposition and real character, but in a *general way* they had a close family resemblance.

I purpose to write of one Blodgett—T. Blodgett, as it was written in the fly-leaf of Webster's Elementary—and he was an extraordinary specimen of the genus pedagogue. But before I introduce him, let me, by way of preface and prelude, give you a view of the salients of the history of the days when pole-ribbed school houses—log cabin school houses—flourished, with each a pedagogue for supreme, "unquestioned and unquestionable" despot.

In those fine days boys from five to fifteen years of age wore tow linen pants held up by suspenders (often made of tow strings), and having at each side pockets that reached down to about the wearer's knees. These pockets held as much as a moderate sized bushel basket will now. The girls, big and little, wore mere tow linen slips, that hung loose from the shoulders. Democracy, pure and undefiled, flourished like a green buckeye tree. Society was in about the same condition as a boy is when his voice is changing. You know when a boy's voice is changing if you hear him in another room getting his lesson by saying it over aloud, you think there's about fourteen girls, two old men, and a dog barking in the room. Society was much the same. The elements of everything were in it, but not developed and separated yet. Women rode behind their husbands on the same horse, occasionally reaching round in the man's lap to feel if the baby was properly fixed. Sometimes the girls rode to singing school behind their sweethearts. At such times the horses always kicked up, and, of course, the girls had to hold on. The boys liked the holding on part. Young men went courting always on Saturday night. The girls wouldn't suffer any hugging before eleven o'clock—unless the old folk were remarkably early to bed. Candles were scarce in those days, so that billing and cooing was done by very dim fire-light. *O, le bon temps!* I've forgot whether that's Latin or French.

The pedagogue was the intellectual and moral centre of the neighborhood. He was of higher authority, even in the law, than the Justice of the Peace. He was consulted on all subjects, and, as a rule, his decisions were final, and went upon the people's record as law. His jurisdiction was unlimited, as to subject matter or amount, and, as to the person, was unquestioned. Of course his territory was bounded by the circumstances of each particular case.

I just now recollect quite a number of pedagogues who in turn ruled me in my youthful days. Of one of them I never think without feeling a strange sadness steal over me. He was a young fellow whom to know was to love; pale, delicate, tender-hearted. He taught us two terms and we all thought him the best teacher in the world. He was so kind to us, so gentle and mild-voiced, so prone to pat us on our heads and encourage us. Some of the old people found fault with him because, as they alleged, he did not whip us enough, but we saw no force in the objection. Well, he took a cough and began to fail. He dismissed us one fine May evening and we saw him no more alive. We all followed him, in a solemn line, to his grave, and for a long time thereafter we never spoke of him except in a low, sad whisper. As for me, till long afterwards, the hushed wonder of his white face haunted my dreams. I have now in my possession a little bead money-purse he gave me.

Blodgett came next, and here my story properly begins. Blodgett—who, having once seen him, could ever forget Blodgett? Not I. He was too marked a man to ever wholly fade from memory. He was, as I have said, a perfect type of his kind, and his kind was such as should not be sneered at. He was one of the humble pioneers of American letters. He was a character of which our national history must take account. He was one of the vital forces of our earlier national growth. He was in love with learning. He considered the matter of imparting knowledge a mere question of effort, in which the physical element preponderated. If he couldn't talk or read it into one he took a stick and mauled it into him. This mauling method, though somewhat distasteful to the subject, always had a charming result—red eyes, a few blubbers and a good lesson. The technical name of this method was "*Warming the Jacket.*" It always seemed to me that the peewee birds sang very dolefully after I had had my jacket warmed. I recollect my floggings at school with so much aversion that I do think, if a teacher should whale one of my little ruddy-faced boys, I'd spread his (the teacher's) nose over his face as thin as a rabbit skin! I'd run both his eyes into one and chew his ears off close to his head, sir! Forgive my earnestness, but I can't stand flogging in schools. It's brutal.

From the first day that Blodgett came circulating his school "articles" among us, we took to him by common consent as a wonderfully learned man. I think his strong, wise looking face, and reserved, pompous manners, had much to do with making this impression. We believed in him fully, and for a long time gave him unfaltering loyalty. As for me, I never have wholly withdrawn my allegiance. I look back, even now, and admire him. I sigh, thinking of the merry days when he flourished. I solemnly avow my faith in progress. I know the world advances every day, still I doubt if men and women are more worthy now than they were in the time of the pedagogues. I don't know but what, after all, I am somewhat of a fogy. Any how, I will not, for the sake of pleasing your literary *swallows* —your eclectics of to-day—turn in and berate my dear old Blodgett. In his day men could not and did not skim the surface of things like swallows on a mill pond. They *dived*, and got what they did get from the bottom, and by honest labor. Whenever one of your silk-winged swallows skims past me and whispers progress, I cannot help thinking of Heyne, Jean Paul and—Blodgett. Somehow genius and poverty are great cronies. It used to be more so than it is now. Blodgett was a genius, and, consequently, poor. He was virtuous, and, of course, happy. He was a Democrat and a Hard Shell Baptist, and he might never have swerved from the path of rectitude, even to the extent of a hair's breadth, if it had not been for the coming of a not over scrupulous rival into the neighboring village. But I must not hasten. A little more and I would have blurted out the whole nub of my story. Bear with me. I have nothing of the "lightning calculator" in me. I must take my time.

It has been agreed that biography must include somewhat of physical portraiture. "What sort of looking man was Blodgett?" I will tell you as nearly as I can, but bear in mind it is a long time since I saw him, and, in the meanwhile, the world has been so washed, and combed, and trimmed, and pearl powdered, that one can scarcely be sure he recollects things rightly. The seedy dandy who teaches the free schools of to-day, is, no doubt, all right as things go; but then the way they go—that's it! As for finding some one of these dapper, umbrella-lugging, green-spectacled, cadaverous teachers to compare with our burly Blodgett, the thing is preposterous.

Our pedagogue, when he first came among us, was, as nearly as I can judge, about forty, and a bachelor, tall, raw-boned, lean-faced, and muscular—a man of many words, and big ones, but not over prone to seek audience of the world. To me, a boy of twelve, he appeared somewhat awful, especially when plying the beech rod for the benefit of a future man, and I do still think that something harder than mere sternness slept or woke in and around the lines of his strong, flat jaws—that something sharper than acid shrewdness lurked in his light gray eyes, and that surely a more powerful expression than ordinary brute obstinacy lingered about his firm mouth and smoothly shaven chin.

Blodgett had a mighty body and a mighty will, joined with a self-appreciation only bounded by his power to generate it. This, added to the deep deference with which he was approached by everybody, made him not a little arrogant and despotic—though, doubtless, he was less so than most men, under like circumstances, would have been. His years sat lightly on him. His step was youthful though slouching, his raven hair was bright and wavy, his skin had the tinge of vigorous health, and in truth he was not far from handsome. His voice was nasal, but pleasantly so.

I cannot hope to give you more than a faint idea of the absolute power vested in Blodgett by the men, women and children of the school vicinage; suffice it to say that his view was a *sine qua non* to every neighborhood opinion, his words the basis of neighborhood action in all matters of public interest. If he pronounced the parson's last sermon a failure, at once the entire church agreed in condemning it, not only as a failure but a consummate blunder. If he hinted that a certain new comer impressed him unfavorably, the nincompoop was summarily kicked out of society. In fact, in the pithy phraseology of these latter days, "it was dangerous to be safe" about where he lived.

Thus, for a long time, Blodgett ruled with

an iron hand his little world, with no one to dream of disputing his right or of doubting his capacity, till at length fate let fall a bit of romance into the strong but placid stream of his life, and tinged it all with rose color. He wrote some poetry, but it is obsolete—that is, it is not now in existence. While this streak of romance lasted he looked, for all the world, like a gilt-edged mathematical problem drawn on rawhide.

It was a great event in our neighborhood when Miss Grace Holland, a yellow-haired, blue-eyed, very handsome and well educated young lady from Louisville, Kentucky, came to spend the summer with Parson Holland, our preacher, and the young woman's uncle. Kentucky girls are all sweet. My wife was a Kentucky girl. All the young men fell in love with Miss Holland right away, but it was of no use to them. Blodgett, in the language of your fast youngsters, "shied his castor into the ring," and what was there left for the others but to stand by and see the glory of the pedagogue during the season of his wooing? It would have done your eyes good to see the pedagogue "slick himself up" each Saturday evening preparatory to visiting the parson's. He went into the details of the toilette with an enthusiasm worthy a better result. Ordinarily he was ostentatiously pious and grave, but now his nature began to slip its bark and disclose an inner rind of real mirthfulness, which made him quite pleasant company for Miss Holland, who, though a mere girl, was sensible and old enough to enjoy the many marked peculiarities of the pedagogue.

On Blodgett's side it was love—just the blindest, craziest kind of love, at first sight. As to Miss Holland, I cannot say. One never can precisely say as to a woman; guessing at a woman's feelings, in matters of love, is a little like wondering which makes the music, a boy's mouth or the jewsharp—a doubtful affair.

Great events never come singly. When it rains it pours. If you have seen a bear, every stump is a bear. A few days after the advent of Miss Holland came a pop-eyed, nervous, witty little fellow with a hand press, and started a weekly paper in our village. A newspaper in town! It was startling.

Blodgett from the first seemed not to relish the innovation, but public sentiment had set in too strongly in its favor for him to jeopardize his reputation by any serious denunciations. A real live paper in our midst was no small matter. Everybody subscribed, and so did Blodgett.

It did, formerly, require a little brains to run a newspaper, and in those days an editor was looked upon as nearly or quite as learned and intelligent as a pedagogue; but everybody, however ignorant himself, could not fail to see that one represented progress, the other conservatism, and formerly most persons were Ultra-Conservatives. This, of course, gave the pedagogue a considerable advantage.

Of course Blodgett and the editor soon became acquainted. The latter, a dapper Yankee, full of "get-up-and-snap," and alert to make way for his paper, measured the pedagogue at a glance, seeing at once that a big bulk of strong sense and a will like iron were enwrapped in the stalwart Hoosier's brain. One of two things must be done. Blodgett must be vanquished or his influence secured. He must be prevailed on to endorse the *Star* (the new paper), or the *Star* must attack and destroy him at once.

Meantime the pedagogue grimly waited for an opportunity to demolish the editor. The big Hoosier had no thought of compromise or currying favor. He would sacrifice the little sleek, stuck-up, big-headed, pop-eyed, Roman-nosed Yankee between his thumb nails as he would a flea. Blodgett was a predestinarian of the old school, and was firmly imbedded in the belief that from all eternity it had been fore-ordained that he was to attend to just such fellows as the editor.

Still, the little lady from Louisville took up so much of his time, and so distracted his mind, that no well laid plan of attack could be matured by the pedagogue. But when nations wish to fight it is easy to find a pretext for war. So with individuals. So with the editor and Blodgett. They soon came to open hostilities and raised the black flag. What an uproar it did make in the county!

This war seemed to come about quite naturally. It had its beginning in a debating society, where Blodgett and the editor were leading antagonists. The question debated was, "Which has done more for the cause of human liberty, Napoleon or Wellington?"

Two village men and two countrymen were the jury to decide which side offered the best argument. The jury was out all night and finally returned a split verdict, two of them standing for Blodgett and two for the editor. Of course it was town against country—the villagers for the editor, the country folk for the pedagogue.

"Huzza for the little editor!" cried the town people.

"'Rah for Blodgett!" bawled the lusty country folk.

The matter quickly came to blows at certain parts of the room. Jim Dowder caught Phil Gates by the hair and snatched him over two seats. Sarah Jane Beaver hit Martha Ann Randall in the mouth with a reticule full of hazel nuts. Farmer Heath choked store-keeper Jones till his face was as blue as moderate-like indigo. Old Mrs. Baber pulled off Granny Logan's wig and threw it at 'Squire Hank. But Pete Develin wound the thing up with a most disgraceful feat. He seized a bucket half full of water and deliberately poured it right on top of the editor's head.

This was the beginning of trouble and fun. Some lawsuits grew out of it and some hard fisticuffs. All the country-folk sided with Blodgett—the towns-folk with the editor. The *Star* began to get dim, but the editor, shrewd dog, when he saw how things were turning, at once took up the question of Napoleon *vs.* Wellington in his journal, kindly and condescendingly offering his columns to Blodgett for the discussion.

The pedagogue foolishly accepted the challenge, and thus laid the stones upon which he was to fall. So the antagonists sharpened their goose quills and went at it. In sporting circles the proverb runs: never bet on a man's own trick. Blodgett ought to have known better than to go to the editor's own ground to fight.

I have always suspected that Miss Holland did much to shear our Samson of his strength. She certainly did, wittingly or unwittingly, occupy too much of his time and thought. Poor fellow! he would have given his life for her. He often looked at her, with his head turned a little one side, sadly, thoughtfully, as I have seen a terrier look at a rat hole, as though he half expected disappointment.

The battle in the *Star* began in very earnest. It was a harvest for the shrewd journalist. Everybody took the *Star* while the discussion was going on. Everybody took sides, everybody got mad, and almost everybody fought more or less. Even Parson Holland and the village preacher had high words and ceased to recognize each other. As for the young lady from Louisville, she had little to say about the discussion, though Blodgett always read to her each one of his articles first in MS. and then in the *Star* after it was printed.

Well, finally, in the very height of the war of words, the editor, in one of his articles, indulged in Latin. As you are aware, when an editor gets right down to pan-rock Latin, it's a sure sign he's after somebody. This instance was no exception to the general rule. He was baiting for the pedagogue. The pedagogue swallowed hook and all.

"*Nil de mortuis nisi bonum*," said the editor, "is my motto, which may be freely translated: "If you can't say something good of the dead, keep your tarnal mouth shut about them!"

Blodgett started as he read this, and for a full minute thereafter gazed steadily and inquiringly on vacancy. At length his great bony right hand opened slowly, then quickly shut like a vice.

"I have him! I have him!" he muttered in a murderous tone, "I'll crush him to impalpable dust!" He forthwith went for a small Latin lexicon and began busily searching its pages. It was Saturday evening, and so busily did he labor at what was on his mind, he came near forgetting his regular weekly visit to Miss Holland.

He did not forget it, however. He went; without pointing out to her the exact spot so vulnerable to his logical arrows, he told her in a confidential and confident way that his next letter would certainly make an end of the editor. He told her that, at last, he had the shallow puppy where he could expose him thoroughly. Of course Miss Holland was curious to know more, but, with a grim smile, Blodgett shook his head, saying that to insure utter victory he must keep his own counsel.

The next day, though the Sabbath, was spent by the pedagogue writing his crusher for the *Star*. He wrote it and re-wrote it, over and over again. He almost ruined a Latin grammar and the afore-mentioned lexicon. He worked till far in the night, revising and elaborating. His gray eyes burned like live coals—his jaws were set for victory.

That week was one of intense excitement all over the county, for somehow it had come generally to be understood that the pedagogue's forthcoming essay was to completely defeat and disgrace the editor. Work, for the time, was mostly suspended. The school children did about as they pleased, so that they were careful not to break rudely in upon Blodgett's meditations.

On the day of its issue the *Star* was in great demand. For several hours the office was crowded with eager subscribers, hungry for a copy. The 'Squire and two constables had some trouble to keep down a genuine riot.

The following is an exact copy of Blodgett's great essay:

MR. EDITOR—SIR: This, for two reasons, is my last article for your journal. Firstly: My time and the exigencies of my profession will not permit me to further pursue a discussion which, on your part, has degenerated into the merest twaddle. Secondly: It only needs, at my hands, an exposition of the false and fraudulent claims you make to classical attainments, to entirely annihilate your unsubstantial and wholly undeserved popularity in this community, and to send you back to peddling your bass wood hams and maple nutmegs. In order to put on a false show of erudition, you lug into your last article a familiar Latin sentence. Now, sir, if you had sensibly foregone any attempt at translation, you might, possibly, have made some one think you knew a shade more than a horse; but "whom the gods would destroy they first make mad."

You say, "*De mortuis nil nisi bonum*" may be freely translated, "If you can't say something good of the dead, keep your tarnal mouth shut about them!" Shades of Horace and Praxiteles! What would Pindar or Cæsar say? But

I will not jest at the expense of sound scholarship. In conclusion, I simply submit the following *literal translation* of the Latin sentence in question: "*De*—of, *mortuis*—the dead, *nil*—nothing, *nisi*—but, *bonum*—goods," so that the whole quotation may be rendered as follows—"Nothing (is left) of the dead but (their) goods." This is strictly according to the dictionary. Here, so far as I am concerned, this discussion ends. Your ob't serv't,

T. BLODGETT.

The country flared into flames of triumph. Blodgett's friends stormed the village and "*bully-ragged*" everybody who had stood out for the editor. The little Yankee, however, did not appear in the least disconcerted. His clear, blue, pop-eyes really seemed twinkling with half suppressed joy. Blodgett put a copy of the *Star* into his pocket and stalked proudly, victoriously, out of town.

After supper he dressed himself with scrupulous care and went over to see Miss Holland. Rumor said they were engaged to be married, and I believe they were.

On this particular evening the young lady was enchantingly pretty, dressed in white muslin and blue ribbons, her bright yellow hair flowing full and free down upon her plump shoulders, her face radiant with health and high spirits. She met the pedagogue at the door with more than usual warmth of welcome. He kissed her hand. All that he said to her that evening will never be known. It is recorded, however, that, when he had finished reading his essay to her, she got up and took from her travelling trunk a "Book of Foreign Phrases," and examined it attentively for a time, after which she was somewhat uneasy and reticent. Blodgett observed this, but he was too dignified to ask an explanation.

The "last day" of Blodgett's school was at hand. The "exhibition" came off on Saturday. Everybody went early. The pedagogue was in his glory. He did not know the end was so near. A little occurrence, toward evening, however, seemed to foreshadow it.

Blodgett called upon the stage a bright eyed, ruddy faced lad, his favorite pupil, to translate Latin phrases. The boy, in his Sunday best, and sleekly combed, came forth and bowed to the audience, his eyes luminous with vivacity. The little fellow was evidently precocious—a rapid if not a very accurate thinker —one of those children who always have an answer ready, right or wrong.

After several preliminary questions, very

promptly and satisfactorily disposed of, Blodgett said:

"Now, sir, translate *Monstrum horrendum informe ingens.*"

Quick as lightning the child replied:

"The horrid monster informed the Indians!"

Fury! The face of the pedagogue grew livid. He stretched forth his hand and took the boy by the back of the neck. The curtain fell, but the audience could not help hearing what a flogging the boy got. It was terrible.

Even while this was going on a rumor rippled round the outskirts of the audience—for you must know that the "exhibition" was held under a bush arbor erected in front of the school house door—a rumor, I say, rippled round the outer fringe of the audience. Some one had arrived from the village and copies of the *Star* were being freely distributed. Looks of blank amazement flashed into people's faces. The name of the editor and that of Prof. W——, of Wabash College, began to fly in sharp whispers from mouth to mouth. The crowd reeled and swayed. Men began to talk aloud. Finally everybody got on his feet and confusion and hubbub reigned supreme. The exhibition was broken up. Blodgett came out of the school house upon the stage when he heard the noise.

He gazed around. Some one thrust a copy of the *Star* into his hand.

Poor Blodgett! We may all fall. The crowd resolved itself into an indignation meeting then and there, at which the following extract from the *Star* was read, followed by resolutions dismissing and disgracing Blodgett:

"The following letter is rich reading for those who have so long sworn by T. Blodgett. We offer no comment:

"EDITOR OF THE STAR—DEAR SIR: In answer to your letter requesting me to decide between yourself and Mr. Blodgett as to the correct English rendering of the Latin sentence "*De mortuis nil nisi bonum*," allow me to say that your free translation is a good one, if not very literal or elegant. As to Mr. Blodgett's, if the man is sincere, he is certainly crazy or wofully illiterate; no doubt the latter.

"Very respectfully,

"W——,

"*Prof. Languages, Wabash College.*"

Blodgett walked away from the school house into the dusky June woods. He knew that it was useless to contend against the dictum of a college professor. His friends knew so too, so they turned to rend him. He was dethroned and discrowned forever. He was boarding at my father's then, and I can never forget the haggard, wistful look his face wore when he came in that evening. I have since learned that he went straight from the scene of his disgrace to Miss Holland, whom he found inclined to laugh at him. The next week he collected what was due him and left for parts unknown.

I was over at parson Holland's, playing with his boys.

The game was mumble peg.

I had been rooting a peg out of the ground and my face was very dirty. We were under a cherry tree by a private hedge. Presently Miss Holland came out and began, girl-like, to pluck and eat the half ripe cherries. The wind rustled her white dress and lifted the gold floss of her wonderful hair. The birds chattered and sang all round us; the white clouds lingered overhead like puffs of steam vanishing against the splendid blue of the sky. The fragrance of leaf and fruit and bloom was heavy on the air. The girl in white, the quiet glory of the day, the murmur of the unsteady wind stream flowing among the dark leaves of the orchard and hedge, the charm of the temperature, and over all, the delicious sound of running water from the brook hard by, all harmonized, and in a tender childish mood I quit the game and lolled at full length on the ground, watching the fascinating face of the young lady as she drifted about the pleasant places of the orchard. Suddenly I saw her fix her eyes in a surprised way in a certain direction. I looked to see what had startled her, and there, half leaning over the hedge, stood Blodgett.

His face was ghastly in its pallor, and deep furrows ran down his jaws. His gray eyes had in them a look of longing blended with a sort of stern despair. It was only for a moment that his powerful frame toppled above the hedge, but he is indelibly pictured in my memory just as he then appeared.

"Good-bye, Miss Holland, good-bye."

How dismally hollow his voice sounded! Ah! it was pitiful. I neither saw nor heard of him after that. Years have passed since then. Blodgett is, likely, in his grave, but I never think of him without a sigh.

Yesterday I was in the old neighborhood, and, to my surprise, learned that the old log school house was still standing. So I set out alone to visit it. I found it rotten and shaky, serving as a sort of barn in which a farmer stows his oats, straw and corn fodder. The genius of learning has long since flown to finer quarters. The great old chimney had been torn down or had fallen, the broad boards of the roof, held on by weight poles, were deeply covered with moss and mould, and over the whole edifice hung a gloom—a mist of decay.

I leaned upon a worm fence hard by and gazed through the long vacant side window, underneath which our writing shelf used to be, sorrowfully dallying with memory; not altogether sorrowfully either, for the glad faces of children that used to romp with me on the old play ground floated across my memory, clothed in the charming haze of distance, and encircled by the halo of tender affections. The wind sang as of old, and the bird songs had not changed a jot. Slowly my whole being crept back to the past. The wonders of our progress were all forgotten. And then from within the old school room came a well remembered voice, with a certain nasal twang, repeating slowly and sternly the words:

"*Arma virumque cano;*" then there came a chime of silver tones—"School is out!—School is out!" And I started, to find that I was all alone by the rotting but blessed old throne and palace of the pedagogue.

AN IDYL OF THE ROD.

IT was as pretty a country cottage as is to be found, even now, in all the Wabash Valley, situated on a prominent bluff, overlooking the broad stretches of bottom land, and giving a fine view of the wide winding river. The windows and doors of this cottage were draped in vines, among which the morning glory and the honeysuckle were the most luxuriant; while on each side of the gravelled walk, that led from the front portico to the dooryard gate, grew clusters of pinks, sweet-williams and larkspurs. The house was painted white, and had green window shutters—old fashioned, to be sure, but cosy, homelike and tasty withal. Everything pertaining to and surrounding the place had an air of methodical neatness, that betokened great care and scrupulous order on the part of the inmates.

About the hour of six on a Monday morning, in the month of May, a fine, hearty, intelligent looking lad of twelve years walked slowly up the path which led from the old orchard to the house. He was dressed in loose trowsers of bottle green jeans, a jacket of the same, heavy boots and a well worn wool hat. The boy's shoulders stooped a little, and a slight hump discovered itself at the upper portion of his back. His face was strikingly handsome, being fair, bright, healthful, and marked with signs of great precocity of intellect, albeit it wore just now an indescribable, faintly visible shade, as of innocent perplexity, or, possibly, grief. His mind was evidently not at ease, but the varying shadows that chased each other across the mild depths of his clear, vivacious eyes would have stumped a physiognomist. Between a laugh and a cry, but more like a cry; between defiance and utter shame, but more like the latter; his cheeks and lips took on every shade of pallor and of flush. He shrugged his shoulders as he moved along, and cast rapid glances in every direction, as if afraid of being seen. "Whippoo-tee, tippoo-tee-tee-e!" sang a great cardinal red bird in the apple tree over his head. He flung a stone at the bird with terrible energy, but missed it.

The mistress of the cottage was at this time in the kitchen preparing for the week's washing, for do not all good Hoosier housewives wash on Monday? She was a middle aged, stoutly built, healthy matron, sandy haired, slightly freckled, blue eyed and quick in her movements. Usually smiling and happy, it was painful to see how she struggled now to master the emotions of great grief and sadness that constantly arose in her bosom, like spectres that would not be driven away.

A bright eyed, golden haired lass of sixteen was in the breakfast room washing the dishes and singing occasional snatches from a mournful ditty. It was sad, indeed, to see a cloud of sorrow on a face so fresh and sweet.

Mr. Coulter, the head of the family, and owner of the cottage and its lands, stood near the centre of the sitting room with his hands crossed behind him, gazing fixedly and sadly on the picture of a sweet child holding a white kitten in its lap, which picture hung on the wall over against the broad fire-place. A look of sorrow betrayed itself even in the dark, stern visage of the man. He drew down his shaggy eyebrows and occasionally pulled his grizzled moustache into his mouth and chewed it fiercely. Evidently he was chafing under his grief.

The cottage windows were wide open, as is

the western custom in fine weather, and the fragrance of spice wood and sassafras floated in on the flood tide of pleasant air, while from the big old locust tree down by the fence fell the twittering prelude to a finch's song. A green line of willows and a thin, pendulous stratum of fog marked the way of the river, plainly visible from the west window, and through the white haze flocks of teal and wood ducks cut swiftly in their downward flight to the water. A golden flicker sang and hammered on the gate-post the while he eyed a sparrow-hawk that wheeled and screamed high over head. The dew was like little mirrors in the grass.

The lad entered the kitchen and said to his mother, in a voice full of tenderness, though barely audible:

"Mammy, where's pap?"

"In the front room, Billy," replied the matron solemnly, quaveringly.

Passing into the breakfast room, Billy looked at his sister and a flash of sympathetic sorrow played back and forth from the eyes of one to those of the other; then he went straight into the sitting room and handed something to Mr. Coulter. It was a moment of silence and suspense. Out in the orchard the cherry and apple blooms were falling like pink and white snow.

The man looked down at his boy sadly, sorrowfully, regretfully. He drew his face into a stern frown. The lad looked up into his father's eyes timidly, ruefully, strangely. It was a living tableau no artist could reproduce. It was the moment before a crisis.

"Billy," said the father gravely, "I took your mother and sister to church yesterday."

"Yes, sir," said Billy.

"And left you to see to things," continued the man.

"Yes, sir," replied the boy, gazing through the window at the flicker as it hitched down the gate-post and finally dropped into the grass with a shrill chirp.

"And you didn't water them pigs!"

"O-o-o! Oh, sir! Geeroody! O me! ouch! lawsy! lawsy! mercy me!"

The slender scion of an apple tree, in the hand of Mr. Coulter, rose and fell, cutting the air like a rapier, and up from the jacket of the lad, like incense from an altar, rose a cloud of dust mingled with the nap of jeans. Down in the young clover of the meadow the larks and sparrows sang cheerily; the gnats and flies danced up and down in the sunshine, the fresh soft young leaves of the vines rustled like satin, and all was merry indeed!

Billy's eyes were turned upward to the face of his father in appealing agony; but still the switch, with a sharp hiss, cut the air, falling steadily and mercilessly on his shoulders.

All along the green banks of the river the willows shook their shining fingers at the lifting fog, and the voices of children going by to the distant school smote the sweet May wind.

"Whippee! Whippee-tippee-tee!" sang the cardinal bird.

"O pap! ouch! O-o-o! I'll not forget to water the pigs no more!"

"S'pect you won't, neither!" said the man.

The wind, by a sudden puff, lifted into the room a shower of white bloom petals from a sweet apple tree, letting them fall gracefully upon the patchwork carpet, the while a ploughman whistled plaintively in a distant field.

"Crackee! O pap! ouch! O-o-o! You're a killin' me!"

"Shet your mouth 'r I'll split ye to the backbone in a second! Show ye how to run off fishin' with Ed Jones and neglect them pigs! Take every striffin of hide off 'n ye!"

How many delightful places in the woods, how many cool spots beside the murmuring river, would have been more pleasant to Billy than the place he just then occupied! He would have swapped hides with the very pigs he had forgot to water.

"O, land! O, me! Geeroody me!" yelled the lad.

"Them poor pigs!" rejoined the father.

Still the dust rose and danced in the level jet of sunlight that fell athwart the room from the east window, and the hens out at the barn cackled and sang for joy over new laid eggs stowed away in cosy places.

At one time during the falling of the rod the girl quit washing the dishes, and thrusting her head into the kitchen said, in a subdued tone:

"My land! Mammy, ain't Bill a gittin' an awful one this load o' poles?"

"You're moughty right!" responded the matron, solemnly.

Along toward the last Mr. Coulter tip-toed at every stroke. The switch actually screamed through the air. Billy danced and bawled and made all manner of serio-comic faces and contortions.

"Now go, sir," cried the man, finally tossing the frizzled stump of the switch out through the window. "Go now, and next time I'll be bound you water them pigs!"

And, while the finch poured a cataract of melody from the locust tree, Billy went.

Poor boy! that was a terrible thrashing, and to make it worse, it had been promised to him on the evening before, so that he had been dreading it and shivering over it all night!

Now, as he walked through the breakfast room, his sister looked at him in a commiserating way, but on passing through the kitchen he could not catch the eye of his mother.

Finally he stood in the free open air in front of the saddle closet. It was just then that a speckled rooster on the barn yard fence flapped his wings and crowed lustily. A turkey cock was strutting on the grass by the old cherry tree.

Billy opened the door of the closet. "A boy's will is the wind's will, and the thoughts of youth are long, long thoughts." Billy peeped into the saddle closet and then cast a glance around him, as if to see if any one was near.

At length, during a pleasant lull in the morning wind, and while the low, tenderly mellow flowing of the river was distinctly audible, and the song of the finch increased in volume, and the bleating of new born lambs in the meadow died in fluttering echoes under the barn, and while the fragrance of apple blooms grew fainter, and while the sun, now flaming just a little above the eastern horizon, launched a shower of yellow splendors over him from head to foot, he took from under his jacket behind a doubled sheep skin with the wool on, which, with an ineffable smile, he tossed into the closet. Then, as the yellow flicker rose rapidly from the grass, Billy walked off, whistling the air of that once popular ballad—

"O give me back my fifteen cents,
And give me back my money," &c.

www.ingramcontent.com/pod-product-compliance
Lightning Source LLC
LaVergne TN
LVHW011219110826
845150LV00006B/1475
9781425516406